THE
KIWI
TARGET

BOOKS BY JOHN BALL

Singapore
Chief Tallon and the S.O.R.
Ananda—Where Yoga Lives
Trouble for Tallon
Then Came Violence
Copcade (editor)
The Murder Children
The Killing in the Market
Police Chief
The Mystery Story (editor)
The Eyes of Buddha
The Winds of Mitamura
Mark One—The Dummy
The Fourteenth Point
Five Pieces of Jade
The First Team
Last Plane Out
Johnny Get Your Gun
Miss 1000 Spring Blossoms
Dragon Hotel
Rescue Mission
The Cool Cottontail
In the Heat of the Night
Arctic Showdown
Judo Boy
Edwards: USAF Flight Test Center
Spacemaster One
Operation Springboard
Records for Pleasure

THE KIWI TARGET

JOHN BALL

Carroll & Graf Publishers, Inc.
New York

Copyright © 1989 by Patricia Ball

All rights reserved

First Carroll & Graf edition 1989

Carroll & Graf Publishers, Inc.
260 Fifth Avenue
New York, NY 10001

Library of Congress Cataloging-in-Publication Data

Ball, John Dudley, 1911–
  The kiwi target / John Ball.
   p. cm.
  ISBN 0-88184-514-0 : $15.95
  I. Title.
PS3552.A455K59 1989
813'.54—dc20   89-15693
                   CIP

Manufactured in the United States of America

For two of New Zealand's finest:

Chief Superintendent James F. Glynn
and
Senior Sergeant C.R. O'Hara

CHAPTER 1

Despite the early hour, the invitation of October springtime was already in the air as Constable Eldon Perkins stood outside the Auckland Airport International Terminal and nourished his spirit on the fresh warm breeze. He was an impressionable young man, and as he looked across the open field where the flight from Sydney would shortly come in, he wished that he too could enjoy some of the magic of faraway places.

At twenty-one, he was only a short while out of the ranks of the police cadets. Only five feet eight and almost too slender for his own good health, he would have been hard pressed in any kind of a physical contest. As was the policy in New Zealand, he was unarmed, depending principally on the authority of his uniform and the warrant card in his pocket to back up his role as a policeman. Concealed in his trousers he did have a very short wooden truncheon that he could resort to in an extreme emergency, but he knew that its efficiency was very limited. The time that it would take to get it out of its deep pocket and to wrap its leather thong around his wrist made it even more impotent.

Constable Perkins was similar to many of the other very young men in the police except in one particular way: he had a phenomenal memory for names and faces. Each morning when he came to work he carefully reviewed the standing file of wanted persons and scanned their portraits. This was not so much to refresh his memory as to bring him up to date on apprehensions and new additions to the lists.

Now as he stood just outside the passenger doors and filled his lungs with the welcome tonic of springtime, Perkins knew that the next hour would be a busy one. In addition to the Qantas flight from Australia, a United 747 coming nonstop from Los Angeles was due in with almost a full load.

When the incoming flight from Sydney was due on the blocks in less than ten minutes, Perkins went back inside the terminal and took his station with two more experienced constables to assist them as might be necessary.

Shortly after the high-pitched howls of the jet engines ceased, the passengers began to come into the terminal. Most of them carried assorted pieces of hand baggage; a few of the more experienced had their passports, arrival forms, and health certificates out and ready. As they passed through the immigration booths, the computer screens visible only to the officers on duty told if each traveler was known to be of any special interest.

Constable Perkins glanced at them all. One face interested him: he caught only a quick glimpse of it in profile, but that was enough. He contrived to move rapidly without attracting attention to a point where he could get a better view. As soon as he had done that, he scanned the other passengers and selected a woman who was carrying her own case, all of the available trolleys being in use. He hurried to her side and relieved her of her bag. "Let me help you," he said, and escorted her outside. After accepting the woman's warm thanks with due modesty, he hurried to the small police office inside the terminal and got on the phone.

His call was quickly fed through to Senior Sergeant Bob O'Hara. "Perkins at the airport," he reported. "Qantas flight from Sydney just in. Among the passengers was Edward Riley, posted as wanted in both Australia and Hong Kong. He's shaved his beard and dyed his hair. He took a taxi from the airport."

Senior Sergeant O'Hara knew all about Perkins and what to expect. "The license number of the cab?" he asked.

Perkins supplied it; it had been no trouble at all to memorize it while he was carrying the arriving passenger's bag out to the bus area. The sergeant took immediate action. All patrolling units were quickly notified.

It did not take long to locate the cab and interview the driver. His passenger from the airport had asked to be let off at a corner on Queen Street. That was unusual because he had had a substantial suitcase to carry. The driver had complied, but he had seen no one contact his passenger before he had pulled away.

In the Intelligence Section some rapid work was under way. The full Interpol blue-coded file on Edward Riley was pulled and examined in detail. He had first appeared as a strong-arm enforcer, then as a bank robber and suspected murderer in several parts of the Far East. He had served a prison term in Singapore and was known to have been associated with "Mr. Asia" before that man's death. Hong Kong had also reported him as being involved in heavy narcotics trafficking. Interpol's assessment was *Extremely dangerous, use maximum caution.*

The superintendent in charge was not happy as he absorbed this information. "I hope to God that Perkins was wrong in his identification of this man," he said to the inspector who was his immediate aide.

"So do I," the inspector agreed. "We have enough on our plate as it is."

At that moment the phone rang briefly. He picked it up and took a short call. "The cab driver is downstairs," he reported.

The inspector took the latest available photograph of Riley from the Interpol folder and from a desk drawer extracted several more of the same general type. Then he looked at his superior.

"Let's go get the bad news," the superintendent said, and led the way out of the room.

The cab driver was a middle-aged man in blue walking shorts and a large-size T-shirt that covered his substantial torso. Like

3

most New Zealanders, he had a good opinion of the police and was glad to do what he could to give them a hand.

Before all of the pictures could be laid for his inspection, he picked up the one of Riley. "That's him," he announced. "No mistaking the bloke. I had me a good look at him when he had me put him down on a corner with no one there to meet him."

"Look again and be sure," the inspector advised. "That photo is several years old."

The cab driver asserted his dignity. "I said that was him. And it is."

Meanwhile a careful check by immigration was under way. It was soon determined that one passenger listed on the Qantas flight manifest, a Mr. Arvin Branson, could not be located. He had given his local address as the Southern Pacific Hotel, but he had not checked in and no reservation was being held in his name.

A call to the Commonwealth Police in Sydney produced results within the hour. An Arvin Branson had been located in Melbourne and interviewed by telephone. He reported that his home had been recently burglarized, but he had not been aware that his passport had been taken. Upon request, he checked his personal papers and reported that it was indeed missing.

That was quite enough to satisfy the superintendent. He notified Police Central Headquarters in Wellington, who in turn advised Interpol that Edward Riley was believed to have been seen coming into the country. He also issued a bulletin to all police stations on both the North and South Islands to be on the lookout for Riley, but not to attempt to take him; that would be a job for the Armed Offenders Squad.

When they were once more alone together, the inspector spoke. "Sir, have you any idea why Riley came here? To hide out for a while, perhaps?"

"I don't think so," the superintendent answered. "To put it as our American friends do, he's a professional hit man. There is something—or more likely somebody—that he's after. Right at this moment I have no idea who has hired him or what his target is, and I don't like that fact one damned bit."

4

CHAPTER 2

As he tried to go through the various letters and documents that his secretary had so neatly stacked for him on his desk, Charlie Swarthmore, president of Swarthmore and Stone, was having a hellish time trying to concentrate on his work. Twice within an hour he stopped what he was doing, stared unseeing out of the window at the sunny California lawn, and made a determined effort to defeat the thing that was gnawing at his mind. But it refused to go away. He knew that his normally sound business judgment was being affected, something that irritated him even more.

The first Charles Swarthmore had been a great admirer of Teddy Roosevelt, with the result that from the first, Swarthmore and Stone had considered the environment in every project it had undertaken. Two generations later the results of that policy were paying off handsomely. Ironically that success was responsible for Charlie Swarthmore's intensely uncomfortable state of mind.

Finally he flipped a switch on his intercom. "Will you ask Peter to come in, please?" he said.

Three minutes later, Peter Ferguson came into the big corner office with no idea why he had been summoned.

"Sit down, Peter," Charlie said. "Coffee?"

"Thanks, no—I just had some."

"Cherry Coke, then; I know you like it."

Peter knew better than to decline twice. "Please," he said.

Charlie opened the door to a concealed bar and poured two drinks. He handed one to Peter and then sat down. "How much do you know about corporate raiders?" he asked.

"Largely what I read in *The Wall Street Journal*. I don't think any self-respecting vulture would care for their company."

"You're not alone."

Peter caught his mood. "Recently some British tycoon went after an American company. You probably read about it. He failed, but he cleared a ninety-four-million-dollar profit. To me, that's obscene."

"I couldn't agree more," Charlie said. "Peter, they're after us."

That was stunning news, and the impact took a few moments to sink in. Peter had so far invested six years of his life in Swarthmore and Stone, and a vice presidency didn't seem to be too far into the future. He and Charlie often conferred because they worked well together. "Who is it?" he asked.

"Pricane."

It could hardly have been worse. Pricane Industries was one of the largest and most ruthless conglomerates born of the merger frenzy that had been in high gear for some time. As one ousted executive had put it, "If Pricane comes after you, grab whatever you can and run for the exits."

Peter ignored his drink. "Pricane wants to buy us out," he said by way of confirmation.

"Yes."

"But you hold a controlling interest—at least, that's what I understand."

Swarthmore leaned back in his chair and folded his hands behind his head. "I wish to hell that I did," he said. "But I don't, not since we went public. Pricane has been buying us up through straw men and street-address accounts for the past two months. I only just got wind of it. Stupid of me, but I didn't see it coming."

"Then we'd better get out proxy solicitations as of now," Peter said. "I know it will cost, but we've got to protect ourselves."

Swarthmore shook his head. "I'm afraid it's too late for that, Peter. Pricane is very good at covering their tracks. We've got only one hope, and that's Bishop."

This time Peter reached for his drink. "I never heard of him."

Charlie rotated his shoulders for a moment to ease the muscular tension. "When Stone pulled out some years ago, it was perfectly amiable; his decision entirely. He sold a block of his stock to a man named Bishop, took his profit, and got out of the picture. Apparently he knew he had terminal cancer."

"What about the rest of his stock?"

"His family sold it on the open market when we went public. Bishop hung on to his."

"Then we'd better get on to Bishop, and fast," Peter said. "Unless you're going to tell me that he sits on Pricane's board, or something like that."

Charlie straightened up and faced Peter across the desk. "I'll tell you all I know about him. He lives in New Zealand, but we don't have an address. All contacts are through his attorney, a man called Raymond O'Malley. Bishop, apparently, is a Howard Hughes type who treasures his privacy. And I gather he can afford it."

"First name?"

"Alfred. That's it, period."

Peter was thinking swiftly. "Have you met O'Malley?"

"No. but he's in good standing, I checked on that."

"If he likes privacy so much, he may not care to have Pricane take over his shares in us without his approval."

Charlie got up and began to walk around his office, something he often did when he had a decision to make. "Peter, you have a New Zealand connection, I seem to recall."

Peter stayed in his chair; as close as he felt to his boss, it wasn't his office. "My mother was born there," he said. "When she married my father, he brought her back here. I was born about two years after that."

"Then she must have—"

Peter interrupted by shaking his head. "I was five when she died: leukemia. After that, Dad never spoke of her; it hurt him too much. I've got a few pictures, one or two keepsakes she brought with her—that's all."

"I'm not trying to pry, Peter."

"That's all right. I lost my father three years ago, about the same time I was divorced."

Charlie picked up a pen from his desk set and then replaced it again. "Have you got any contacts in New Zealand? Relatives, perhaps?"

"My mother had a sister, but we've never been in touch. That's about it. I have no idea where she is now."

7

Swarthmore thought for another few seconds before he declared himself. "Peter, as things stand, whether or not we're going to be able to survive as an independent company depends on Bishop. I've talked to the attorney, O'Malley, on the phone. He was courteous, but he wouldn't give out any information.

"I want you to go to New Zealand, before the end of the week if possible, and sit down with O'Malley. See what you can do on a face-to-face basis. Since I may be spending Pricane's money, I'll pop for first class."

"You're putting a lot of trust in me," Peter said.

"I know," Charlie answered, "but if I had any doubts, I'd send someone else. Do you mind?"

"No," Peter answered. "You've put me on the ropes for the moment, that's all."

Charlie visibly relaxed a little. "Pricane may be there ahead of you, so get to O'Malley as fast as you can. I'd suggest that you go as a tourist: look around the country a little. Pricane has long ears, so keep your business connections to yourself, except with O'Malley. And Bishop, of course, if you get the chance."

"I think it would look better if you went yourself," Peter said.

"I don't dare. The name Swarthmore is too conspicuous, particularly right now. Your name shouldn't tip anyone off, in case Pricane has their antennae out."

"I see the point of that," Peter agreed. "My name won't ring any warning bells."

As far as he knew, that was a true and accurate statement.

CHAPTER 3

The first major reaction that Peter had as he walked outside the Auckland terminal, pushing a cart with his luggage, was gratitude that he was in an English-speaking country. Since this was the first time he had been abroad, he had a firm desire to do things properly, right from the beginning. Customs varied, he knew that, and he could not afford to make mistakes anywhere along the line. There was far too much at stake for that.

The next taxi driver in line was a firmly built man of about fifty who was standing beside his vehicle. He wore an open cotton shirt and a pair of walking shorts that barely covered the tops of his muscular legs. "Here, let me have a go at that," he said, and took over the luggage cart with swift efficiency. He loaded Peter's two suitcases onto the back seat and shut the door. "You can ride up with me," he added.

If that was the way they did things in New Zealand, all right, Peter thought. He dutifully tried to get in on the right-hand side and then realized his mistake. The driver took it in stride. "A lot of you Americans do that," he said. "We drive on the left, you see." He waited while Peter walked around and got in, then started up and pulled onto the exit road. "Where to?" he asked.

"The Southern Pacific Hotel."

"That's a good choice, right at the foot of Queen Street. Convenient to everything. Your first visit here?"

"Yes."

"Welcome to kiwi land. That's what we call ourselves—kiwis. After the little bird that can't fly."

Once he was in his hotel room, Peter stripped and took a reviving shower that washed away some of his fatigue. Despite a tempting look at the comfortable bed, he dressed and put through a call to the office of Raymond O'Malley.

It took a few minutes for the connection; then O'Malley's secretary came on the line. Her voice was rich with accent. "Mr. O'Malley knows of your visit, Mr. Ferguson," she reported. "Unfortunately, he's entirely tied up for the rest of the week. He left word that if it's convenient for you, he can meet with you in Queenstown for lunch on Saturday."

Peter had no idea where Queenstown was, but there was no doubt about keeping the appointment. "I'll be there, of course," he said.

"I'll inform Mr. O'Malley. He has suggested that you might

put up at the Mountaineer Establishment. He knows the management very well, and they'll take good care of you."

"Thank you. Will I need a reservation?"

"I'll be glad to make one for you. There's a direct flight on Mount Cook Airlines. Where are you staying?"

"At the Southern Pacific in Auckland."

"The booking office for Mount Cook is just around the corner. I'd suggest that you check in with them as soon as possible. The Queenstown flights are usually filled up early."

Shortly thereafter, the receptionist at the Southern Pacific Hotel answered a police inquiry by confirming that Mr. Peter Ferguson had arrived and checked in. He had asked the way to the Mount Cook office and had presumably gone there. He had returned after a short while and was believed to be resting in his room.

The Mount Cook office, in turn, advised that he had purchased a ticket for Queenstown, one of the principal tourist Meccas on the South Island, and was holding a reservation on the morning flight.

The small police station at Queenstown was then informed that a Mr. Peter Ferguson was expected to arrive the following day. No action was required, but all readily available information concerning his activities was desired.

In the early morning light with a vaulting blue sky overhead, the world headquarters of Pricane Industries was a spectacular sight. The central tower soared upward almost fifty stories, to be crowned by the blue and white symbol that was seen in every office and on every piece of literature of the huge conglomerate. It was one of the largest such complexes in the central United States.

The forty-fifth floor and above housed the very heart of Pricane management, a rarefied atmosphere restricted to a chosen few. The president's suite occupied most of the forty-ninth floor. The president himself, who was in his late fifties, had been brought in some five years before, in part to augment the Pricane

10

image of dynamic progress. When he had been photographed bare-chested on his yacht, he had projected a virile image in the company of the Playmate of the Year.

The office suite of Reinhold Lloyd was on the forty-eighth floor. On the complex organizational chart he appeared near the top, as vice president in charge of new development. When he shook hands, he often seemed an easy man with whom to deal. If he had any questions to ask, he put them in a quiet, emotionless voice. When he reached a decision, he invariably gave his answer in a soft yes or no.

Those who had not known better had sometimes tried to debate a point. It was then they learned what manner of man Lloyd was. It was said that one lesser executive had suffered a cardiac seizure in his office. Yet Lloyd could make himself quite pleasant if he chose to do so.

In his outer office Mrs. DeForest looked up when a stranger to her came in. She noted at once that his clothes were expensive, although probably made overseas, and that he had a distinct executive aura. He was tall enough to be impressive and very trim in his build.

No one reached Lloyd's office without her advance knowledge. She gave a brief ring on the intercom. If he did not answer, she would not disturb him again without permission.

"Yes?"

"Mr. Kincaid is here."

She listened a brief moment and then gave her usual formal smile to the well-tanned man who was waiting. "Please go right in, Mr. Kincaid." She led the way to the inner door and held it open for him.

Lloyd came from behind his desk to shake hands, which was definitely unusual. "Sit down, Ted," he invited, and waved toward a chair in the corner of the large office. "How was São Paulo?"

Kincaid smiled. "A great city. I enjoyed it."

"Four years, wasn't it?"

Kincaid nodded. "Just about." It had actually been a little over five, but that didn't matter; what did was the fact that he had

11

successfully walked the tightrope between correcting Lloyd, which was unthinkable, and endorsing a misstatement.

"I called you back because I've got something new I want to put you on," Lloyd said, still maintaining his agreeable manner. "You got good results in Brazil: I've reviewed them."

"Thank you."

"Any thought on who might succeed you down there?"

It was a clear trap that Kincaid saw at once. Undoubtedly Lloyd knew that he and Jack Bernstein were close friends, but there was no place for sentiment at Pricane.

"I left Bernstein in charge; he can handle it until you choose my replacement."

"For how long?"

"As long as necessary." That was the best he could do for his friend. He was taking a chance as it was, because Lloyd was rumored not to like Jews.

Lloyd wasted no more time; Kincaid had passed. "Ted, we're about to acquire a very good company, Swarthmore and Stone. Real estate and developments. So far we've kept it very sub rosa."

Kincaid listened silently.

"We're rounding up all the stock and proxies we'll need. As soon as that's done, they'll have a board meeting, at which time you'll be elected president and chief executive officer."

Kincaid nodded at that but nothing more.

"We can keep this acquisition under wraps for three months because we're using straw men. And since you've been away for a while, you aren't known as a Pricane executive."

"I could offer my resignation from São Paulo, just in case," Kincaid said.

"That's already been handled."

A sharp sense of annoyance touched Kincaid, but he managed to keep it from showing.

Lloyd went on. "Right now we're after two things. There's a man in New Zealand, a recluse named Bishop, who holds a significant block of stock in Swarthmore and Stone. We want his stock or his proxy—it doesn't really matter which one. We'll get the stock later in any case."

12

"Can we acquire the company without him?" Kincaid asked.

Lloyd pressed his lips together. "Right now he has a controlling interest, or close enough to it to be a nuisance. We're willing to buy him out at well over market, which is probably what he's after. I want you to handle that."

Kincaid nodded.

"While you're down there, look around for any desirable potential developments. Later, as president of Swarthmore and Stone, you'll be in a prime position to negotiate for the necessary properties. If Bishop is at all difficult, you might make some trade-offs."

"What's my position?"

Lloyd approved of the question.

"You're representing a large block of Swarthmore and Stone stockholders who want our offer accepted. We can back that up with our present holdings. None of them are in our name."

He picked up a black binder that had been placed on the corner table. "Here's all the information you'll need on Swarthmore and Stone, what we have on Bishop, and some fill-in on New Zealand. Apparently, they're pretty primitive down there. Mostly they raise sheep."

Kincaid accepted the binder but avoided looking into it while Lloyd was briefing him. A blunder like that could cost him his new assignment, one that should carry a substantial salary increase.

A light glowed on the phone and Lloyd picked it up. "Yes?"

"The meeting you are to address is in ten minutes."

Lloyd hung up without speaking. "We've learned that Swarthmore and Stone has sent an engineering type to New Zealand to try and see Bishop. Bishop doesn't see anyone. He deals through his attorney; his name's in the file."

Kincaid nodded that he had absorbed everything so far.

"We've been having some image problems lately because of the number of our acquisitions and the way we've been getting them. At the moment we're facing an FTC investigation—another reason we want to keep this totally under cover."

Lloyd let a flash of anger cross his features. "We lost a major

13

deal recently because someone we'd fired peddled our ass to *The Washington Post*. So stay out of sight as much as you can. As soon as we have controlling interest, S and S will become our operating division for New Zealand. You'll continue as president at a hundred and fifty, plus options."

That was beyond Kincaid's expectations; he had hoped for a hundred to a hundred and a quarter.

On his way out, he paused by Mrs. DeForest's desk. He noted the way her knit dress clung to her figure and the way that she looked up at him.

"May I ask a question?" He put it very casually.

"Of course, Mr. Kincaid." She was quite proper, but he caught a possible signal.

"What is the best dinner house in town?"

Wilma DeForest lifted her shoulders and allowed a small smile to show. "If you don't mind driving, Valini's, about fifteen miles north of here, is quiet. The food and service are both very good."

"How about eight o'clock?"

Mrs. DeForest paused just long enough to suggest that she was considering the matter. "Only by accident," she said.

"Of course."

As he left with the black folder held carefully in his hand, Kincaid hoped that the women in New Zealand would be of equally high caliber.

CHAPTER 4

At eight-thirty the following morning Peter was back at the Auckland Airport ready for his flight for Queenstown. When he went out to board the plane, instead of a sleek jet he saw a small, stubby aircraft that could have been built in the sixties.

When it was his turn, Peter climbed inside and discovered that the rows of seats were almost impossibly close together; he had to slide in sideways to take his assigned place next to the rearmost window. When he sat down, there was just room for his knees and no more.

He was still trying to make himself comfortable in the limited space when a very large and bulky man crammed himself into the narrow seat beside him.

The plane taxied out, turned onto the active runway, and accomplished a sedate take-off. It climbed slowly toward the few puffs of cumulus in the sky, refusing to admit that there were other aircraft capable of far better performance and much more comfort.

As the crowded little turboprop droned on, Peter made the best of it and took in what he could see of the countryside. After some time had passed, a range of snow-capped mountains began to come into view. From their general appearance he assumed that they were the famed Southern Alps. A few minutes later, he saw one of them that soared impressively higher than the rest. It had to be Mount Cook, as much a symbol of New Zealand as Fujiyama is of Japan. The aircraft began a descent and shortly thereafter landed on an almost absurdly short runway, one that had obviously not been designed with any thought of jets.

A few passengers deplaned, then others came on board to take their places. There was not a spare seat in the heavily loaded, compact aircraft. Peter's back began to ache, but there was nothing he could do about it since there was no room at all to switch his legs to a more comfortable position.

After the plane had climbed back into the air once more, his seatmate twisted his considerable bulk toward him a little. "It's a nice day to fly, isn't it," he said.

"The weather's fine," Peter agreed, "but this is pretty cramped."

The big man nodded. "None of us like it, but that's the way it is. It's because there's such a demand for seats. This your first trip here?"

Peter told him a brief story about being on vacation and then asked, "What do you do?"

"I've got a station up the lake. A couple thousand sheep and some other things."

15

"It's yours, I take it."

"That's right. Been in the family a long time."

"I don't know your name."

"It's Jack. Jack McHugh."

"Peter Ferguson."

The huge man looked at him with renewed interest. "Is that so, now? Where will you be staying, Peter?"

"At the Mountaineer."

"That's a nice hotel—good food there. After you've settled in, give me a call. I'll have you up at the station to see the place." He wrote on a page in a pocket notebook and then tore it out. "When you get there, I'll take you to the pub," he said as he passed the paper over. "I've some good mates for you to meet."

Peter sensed that his companion wanted to say something more, but the big man apparently thought better of it and left things as they were.

Some time later, as the little airliner was coming in for another landing, he did speak again.

"This'll be Queenstown. Small quiet place, but very nice. Makes its living from the tourists."

As the plane taxied in, Peter noted that the field was minimal and the terminal building, while neat and attractive, was not much larger than a small house.

Once inside, he reclaimed his luggage and went outside to find a cab. The only public vehicle appeared to be a minibus that was rapidly loading up. His temper rose a little: his back ached from the close confinement inside the plane, his luggage was a nuisance, and the line outside the bus already guaranteed it a full load. Then he saw a small sedan waiting in a single-car taxi zone. A girl was standing beside it. "Can you take me to the Mountaineer Establishment?" he asked.

"Of course," she answered.

As he lifted his luggage once more, a fresh spasm is his back caused him a stab of pain. "Then please do," he said, more sharply than he intended.

He put his bags in the back himself and then sat in the left front seat. As the girl pulled away from the terminal, he was

16

aware that she was sitting stiffly and that her hands were tight on the wheel. Either she was a new driver, or else he had offended her.

To ease the situation he asked, "How large is Queenstown?"

"About three thousand." She was definitely distant.

"Tell me about it," he invited.

The girl turned a corner and mellowed a little. "It's quiet. We think it's very beautiful. You might want to try one of the jet boats; most of the tourists like them."

"Any good theaters or shows?"

"Not in Queenstown. This isn't like Las Vegas."

"You've been to the States?" As he spoke, the end of a large and exquisitely blue lake came into view. On the opposite shoreline some quite respectable mountains formed a spectacular backdrop.

"No, I've never been out of New Zealand. But I know about it."

Peter studied her profile for a moment. "I'm sorry if I was abrupt," he said. "I didn't mean to be. I had to ride all the way from Auckland with a very big man beside me. I could hardly move, and I got off with a back cramp."

The girl glanced at him for a moment before she gave her attention back to the road. "Did he give you his name?" she asked.

"Jack McHugh. He said that he owns a station up the lake."

The girl nodded without looking at him again. "He is big. But nice, I think. He's my father."

Embarrassment took hold of him. "You were there to meet him," he said.

"Yes, but I was also hoping for a fare. He doesn't mind the bus."

The girl pulled up in front of a small hotel. Peter got out quickly to be sure that he handled his own bags; he would be damned if he let her do that. "Please tell your father that I enjoyed his company," he said as he handed over a bill.

"I'll tell him." The girl gave him back his exact change and drove off without any suggestion that she would accept a tip.

The Mountaineer made no attempt to be pretentious, but it had an inviting atmosphere. As soon as he had registered, Peter turned to find a quite young man waiting to speak to him. "We're glad to have you with us, Mr. Ferguson," he said, and handed over a card. "Please call me personally if there is anything at all we can do for you." There was an undertone to the words that Peter could not quite grasp. He knew that he was being given a VIP welcome, but the reason for it eluded him.

Up a flight of stairs he was shown into a well-furnished and comfortable room. As he refreshed himself he had thoughts of eating, but he wasn't yet hungry. Instead, he left the hotel to explore Queenstown. Inevitably the lake drew him. He took the short walk to the shoreline and found a bench where he could sit and allow himself to respond to its beauty.

Lake Wakatipu was indeed a magnificent sight. Its color was an intense blue, while across the water the Remarkables rose upward in unspoiled grandeur. The air was brillantly clear except for a thin feather of smoke that was drifting upward from the stack of an ancient steamer docked a block away. A cluster of small boats, some bearing the names of stations up the lake, were tied up alongside a convenient pier.

Aware that he needed it, he put everything else aside to enjoy the wonderful sense of space and openness. After a few minutes he was infused with the feeling that he wanted all this to remain as it was. Developers would be sure to come in to build condominiums and speed up the pace of life. It would all generate substantial profits, and that was the name of the game, but as he sat looking at the unspoiled vista of the whole magnificent scene, he wished it were not so inevitable.

If Pricane or some other equally ruthless combine ever discovered this wonderland, it would end up looking like the Tamiami Trail south from Miami, and the very thought of that made him shudder.

God willing, he would have to get to Bishop as fast as he possibly could.

CHAPTER 5

At a few minutes after 10 P.M., Constable Grady pulled his patrol unit into the parking lot of the R and R Lodge and got out to pay his usual visit to the landlord. He did not always arrive at the same hour, but he could be depended upon to stop in sometime during the evening. It was through such visits that the New Zealand police picked up a great deal of useful information.

The bar was comfortably full, which was good for Henry Cartright, the owner. Henry was well liked, both for himself and because he ran a very orderly establishment that suited almost everyone in that particular area of the South Island. It was more than fifteen miles to Nelson, the nearest city, so the R and R's trade was largely made up of local regulars and a certain number of visiting fishermen who put up at the lodge, most of them year after year.

When the figure of Constable Grady appeared in the doorway, his arrival was duly noted. He walked once through the large room exchanging nods with a number of the patrons. Everything was in good order, as he knew it would be; he was there largely in case anyone wanted to speak to him.

Someone did. Behind the bar, and with a long neat row of inverted bottles in dispensing holders behind him, the landlord gave him a slight sign that he had something to say. Constable Grady walked over and accepted the half pint of potent New Zealand beer that was set before him.

The landlord rested his elbows on the bar and spoke without being conspiratorial. "Had an odd one today," he said. "Couple of chaps stopped in here and offered to buy the place."

Constable Grady tasted his beer and set the mug down. "Didn't know you were thinking of selling, Henry."

"I'm not, and never let anyone think so."

"What sort of chaps?"

"Well, that's it. They were Aussies. You know that most Aussies are right fine chaps, but these two didn't strike me as quite the sort of chums I'd care to have—or my customers, either."

"What did you tell them?"

"I thanked them but said no way I'm going to sell. The Mrs. and I've been here twenty-two years in October. It's the kind of life we like. Plenty of friends and a good income. Enough for all we want and more."

When he completed his patrol, Constable Grady included mention of the incident in his report. He saw nothing wrong in the offer to buy the lodge, but he thought it odd that it had come from men not known to the landlord. Proper buyers would have wanted to see the place first.

The senior sergeant who read the report the following day had been advised to note any items pertaining to Australians in general and to one Edward Riley in particular. Therefore he showed the report very promptly to the inspector in charge.

The inspector, who had been given certain additional information, made an immediate call to the district superintendent. The superintendent listened and gave the inspector some specific instructions. An official OHMS* envelope was also sent to him by urgent transit.

When the inspector received the envelope, he left as soon as he conveniently could for the R and R Lodge to interview the landlord. He was received during closed time, which was no problem for a policeman. When he laid out a collection of ten photographs for the landlord to see, Cartright did not hesitate in picking out two of them. He was very definite in his identification and agreed that he could swear to it in court.

The inspector asked to use the telephone without having to add that he would appreciate some privacy.

"I'm at the R and R," he reported to the superintendent. "The landlord has given a positive identification of the two men who called on him. I was sure you'd be interested."

"What are the photo numbers?" the superintendent asked.

"Two and eight."

"Ah!" The superintendent was very pleased. "I'd like to inter-

* On Her Majesty's Service

view those gentlemen myself as soon as possible, especially Mr. Riley."

"I'll try to see to it," the inspector said.

Two days later, at a little after three in the morning, Henry Cartright suddenly sat up in bed. He thought he detected the odor of smoke, and it had been enough to awaken him. He sniffed carefully and then almost jumped out of bed. He climbed into his trousers and woke his wife at the same time. When he opened the door seconds later, the pungent odor was suddenly stronger, and he knew the worst. "Fire!" he barked, and then ran down the stairs as fast as he could.

The taproom was already blazing fiercely in one corner, and he could see that the fire was spreading rapidly. He kept his head; his wife would rouse the other sleepers on the premises. The most effective thing he could do was to phone for help.

Less than a minute later, the nearest fire units were on their way, but they had a long distance to come.

The call made, Cartright ran to the closest fire barrel, seized the pail, and began to throw one bucketful after another onto the flames. If anything, it seemed to spread the fire even faster. When he had emptied the barrel and could do no more at that spot, he took in a deep breath of much-needed air. As he did so, he detected the sharp odor of kerosene.

He saw that two other men were also fighting the fire, but it was hopeless. He ran outside and stood with his wife, where he watched his home, his livelihood, and all his possessions give way to the flames. He could have endured it if it had been an accident, but he knew as he knew night from day that the fire had been deliberately set, that his property was being willfully destroyed.

He was standing back from the fire, shaking with rage, when he heard the siren of the first approaching engine. The lads were coming, but they were too late: there was nothing then that could be saved.

When he awoke in the morning, Peter shaved, showered, and

21

dressed casually, which was obviously correct for Queenstown. He had two days to wait for his appointment with O'Malley, but in this restful vacation spot that would be no hardship. And there was always the chance that the attorney might call him and move up the time of their meeting.

Once more he walked over toward the shoreline, sat on the same bench, and wondered what it would be like to live in a place like this. To him, New Zealand had always been the distant and dimly imagined place from which his mother had come. Now it was a vivid reality, toward which he felt a certain affinity that was part of his birthright.

Not ready to eat, Peter walked toward the Travelodge purely out of curiosity. As he entered the lobby, he discovered that it was a center of tourist activity. A huge pile of luggage had been built up in the lobby, scores of people were being herded into the coffee shop for an assembly-line breakfast, and the girls at the check-out counter were furiously busy.

Outside, several large tourist buses were waiting for their loads. Since all this was new to him, he found a place to sit where he could watch without being in the way.

Within the next few minutes, bellhops began to move part of the massive stack of luggage. An announcement was made; in response, a large group of people began to flow outside toward the waiting buses.

After that, it was much calmer. An attractive girl behind a small Mount Cook travel desk began gathering up her papers. He glanced at his watch; it was seven forty-eight, and the coffee shop was clear enough for him to go in now for his own breakfast.

He yielded first to a strong temptation. He got up and walked over to the girl at the travel desk. "I'm going in for some breakfast. Will you join me—at least for a cup of coffee?" he asked.

To his surprise, she accepted. "A cup of tea would be nice."

As she led the way into the coffee shop, Peter noted her figure and her walk and approved of both.

A waitress who was busy clearing up paused at their table. "What'll it be, Jenny?"

"Tea, and maybe a pastry to go with it." She looked at Peter to be sure it was all right.

"And you, sir?"

"I'd like some breakfast."

The waitress glanced at Jenny, who nodded, then she left.

Peter looked at his companion and received a smile that was warm and appealing. "This is very nice of you," she said.

"Believe me, it's my pleasure."

Jenny paused before she spoke again. "Louise McHugh told me about you. She drove you in from the airport."

"I met her father on the plane."

"I know. Jack is very well liked by everybody."

"How did you know me?"

Jenny toyed with a spoon. "This is a very small town. When someone like you comes in, we generally hear about it."

He had a strong feeling that she was holding something back, but he had no idea what it could be. He put it into words. "And what makes me so different?"

The question seemed to disturb her. She looked at him carefully, appraising him, before she answered. "You're FIT, for one thing. Then Louise said that after you were rude to her, you apologized. Most tourists wouldn't."

"What does FIT mean?" he asked.

"Foreign Independent Travel. It means you can afford to travel at full rates, not on a group fare."

He decided to change the tack. "What's your full name?"

"Jenny Holbrook."

"A Queenstown girl?"

"I've lived here all my life."

The waitress arrived carrying a tray. She served Jenny tea and a sweet roll. In front of Peter she put down a plate of scrambled eggs, bacon, fried potatoes, and sliced tomatoes. To that she added a pot of coffee. "Will that do?" she asked.

"It's great," Peter answered. "How did you get it so fast?"

"It's the employees' breakfast; we had it ready."

When she had gone, Jenny broke her roll and ate a small piece. "And your name?" she asked.

"Ferguson, Peter Ferguson." As he spoke, he sensed she had already known what his answer would be.

"Married?"

"Divorced." He quickly changed the subject. "What should I see in Queenstown?" he asked.

"Take the steamer trip up the lake to Walter Peak Station. In the afternoon, take one of the jet boat rides; you'll really like that. I can book for you, if you want me to."

"Thank you," Peter said.

Hardly an hour later, he was on a venerable old steamer plowing a steady trail up the wonderfully clear water of the lake. At the station he watched a sheepdog demonstration and enjoyed the elaborate morning tea that was served as though the fee-paying tourists were invited guests.

The jet boat ride was a dramatic experience as it skimmed close to overhanging rocks at high speed and performed some of the startling maneuvers of which it was capable. When it spun around in a way impossible for an ordinary craft, some of the passengers screamed, as they always did.

Sergeant Bill Woodley, who was in charge of the small police detachment in Queenstown, was young for his rank, but he had earned it through efficient performance. On the same morning that Peter took the steamer excursion, Sergeant Woodley had a brief conversation with Louise McHugh.

"When I picked him up at the airport, I didn't know that his name was Peter Ferguson," she told him. "He didn't identify himself, and I didn't ask."

"Quite understood. What was your impression of him?"

"At first I didn't like him at all; he was very short with me. Then on the way in he asked me some questions about Queenstown—what kind of a place it was and if there were any theaters here."

"I see. Would you say that they were casual tourist inquiries, or something more?"

"Neither one; he was just trying to make conversation. Then, very nicely, he apologized. I can't remember anybody else doing that. Of course I thought much better of him then."

"Suppose you met again and he asked you for a date."

Louise understood just what Bill Woodley meant. "I might," she said.

The sergeant next stopped at the Mountaineer Establishment. "Mr. Ferguson is a good guest," the manager told him. "He conducts himself well, and he's considerate of the staff."

"From your observation, do you think he knows?"

"I doubt it. If you'd asked me, I'd have said it was a coincidence."

Woodley left with a policeman's inherent dislike of coincidences still in his mind. He returned to the police office and rang through to Jack McHugh up at his station. The two men knew each other well, so McHugh spoke with candor.

"I liked the chap. Not stuffy, not impressed with himself, and kept quiet until I spoke to him. I can't be sure, Bill, but I gathered that either he doesn't know or he's not the right man. It could be either one."

Bill Woodley thanked him, gave the usual injunction about not mentioning any part of the conversation to anyone, and made some additional notes on his pad. He then phoned in a report covering what he had learned. He carefully refrained from offering any opinion of his own, but he still didn't like coincidences.

CHAPTER 6

It was a little after eight-thirty that evening when Ray O'Malley rang through to the Mountaineer Establishment and asked for Peter Ferguson. Since there was no phone in his room, he had to be called down to the lobby, where a private booth was placed at his disposal.

"Mr. Ferguson," O'Malley said, "I must begin by apologizing to you for the inconvenience I know I've put you

25

through. I wouldn't have done it if there'd been any alternative."

Peter was quick on the pick-up. "As a matter of fact, I'm very comfortable here, and Queenstown is a beautiful place. Pending our meeting, I don't feel inconvenienced at all."

"Very generous of you to look at it that way. I appreciate it," O'Malley said. "I believe I understand the purpose of your visit. You're concerned about Mr. Bishop's holding in Swarthmore and Stone. But I don't know your exact position. Are you an attorney, Mr. Ferguson?"

"No, I'm a lead engineer at S and S."

"And a stockholder?"

"Yes, and I hold options for more."

"I see." O'Malley's tone changed a little. "Mr. Ferguson, the reason I called is to advise you that I'm almost hopelessly tied up for the next three or four days. I don't like to be cavalier like this, but I don't have any real choice."

"We've had similar situations," Peter said. No matter what O'Malley was about to tell him, he had to stay on the man's good side.

O'Malley went on. "I'm afraid I've got to cancel our lunch on Saturday. I hope you understand. However, I will meet with you as soon as this crisis is over, I guarantee that."

"Understood," Peter said, and then put his own oar in the water. "I'll be glad to wait until you're free. Meanwhile, can you give me two minutes of your time, right now, on the phone?"

"Of course."

"At the moment our company, Swarthmore and Stone, is directly under the gun of a particularly ruthless corporate raider."

"You mean Pricane Industries?"

"Yes. If they can take over Mr. Bishop's holdings, we're done for. I know you're his attorney and principal adviser."

"That's true."

"I came to New Zealand to present our case to you and, if possible, to Mr. Bishop personally. I'll wait as long as necessary if you'll be kind enough to defer any decision concerning Mr. Bishop's stock until after we've met."

O'Malley hesitated only a moment. "All right, I'll accept that," he said. "May I make a suggestion?"

"Please do."

"You might as well enjoy yourself while you're here. Our West Coast is quite a remarkable, unspoiled region. I'll arrange a rental car for you if you'd like to drive over to see it. By the time you're back, we should be able to sit down together."

"It's a deal," Peter said.

The police investigation at the site of the R and R Lodge was prompt and thorough. The ashes had hardly cooled before an expert team went to work. Within an hour definite evidence was found confirming that it was a case of arson. Once that was established, a number of other avenues of investigation were opened up.

Every regular patron of the Lodge was interviewed, while Henry Cartright, the licensee, was talked with at length. It was very quickly proven that the business had been sound and profitable, so any question of deliberate destruction for the sake of the insurance was ruled out.

After all of this work had been done, there was a conference that included Constable Grady, who had the most intimate knowledge of the area and the people concerned; Sergeant Tapui, a Maori, who had done much of the field work; and Inspector Roderick Jones, who was in charge of the investigation.

When tea had been set out all around from the serviceable if not elegant facilities at the station, Jones called on Grady first for his opinion.

"I can't see Cartright involved in arson," he said. "The evidence is all against it. Also, I've known the man for some time, and I'd vouch for him."

"I agree," Sergeant Tapui said.

"The insurance people are of the same opinion," Inspector Jones added. "So I think we can take it as given that Mr. Cartright is not our arsonist."

"Also, sir," Grady added, "I believe we can exclude local residents, as well as the regular patrons of the Lodge."

In his report Inspector Jones set down the details of the investigation and added the opinion that no local people had been responsible for the arson. Since the two Australians who had called at the pub shortly before the fire both had extensive criminal records, suspicion pointed very strongly toward them.

The superintendent who reviewed it concurred. The word was passed to all stations to be on the alert for the wanted men. If located, they were to be handled with maximum care.

While sitting quietly in a corner of the Mountaineer bar, Peter did some careful thinking. He was definitely upset by the delay in seeing O'Malley; his mind kept conjuring up various disasters that could occur before he could complete his mission. At the same time, he could see a benefit: by keeping him waiting this way, O'Malley was being put under a certain obligation.

He had agreed to listen to what Peter had to say. He might even pave the way for a personal meeting with Bishop. If that became a reality, then any delay would be justified.

As far as going up the West Coast was concerned, he was not too enthusiastic. Queenstown was an ideal place to rest and wait. Also, in the back of his mind he had the thought of asking Jenny Holbrook out.

But O'Malley had suggested the West Coast trip; if he turned the idea down, it might not sit too well. O'Malley had even offered to arrange for a car. Obviously, he had no choice: thank God he had had enough sense to see that.

In the morning a solid breakfast and three cups of coffee got him in gear for the day. He packed his bags, checked out, and was waiting when a little red Ford Cortina pulled up in the small parking lot.

The road map was simplicity itself—a sheet of paper that showed the single highway up the West Coast of the South Island and the few other roads that fed into it.

"There's a government-owned tourist hotel at Franz Josef, where you may want to spend the night," the driver said. "Take care on the one-way bridges, and have a fine trip."

At first, Peter found driving on the left unexpectedly trying. Staying on what was to him the wrong side of the road was bad enough, but because he was seated on the right side of his vehicle, all his feeling for clearances was thrown off. Twice he ran the left tires off the road before he began to get a better command of the car.

Following the map he had been given, he took a narrow, winding road to Wanaka, where he turned westward. When he finally cleared the last of the winding turns and saw the brilliant, tumbling, almost living waters of the Tasman Sea, all of his long-suppressed sense of wanderlust came surging back.

He marveled at the magnificent, unspoiled panorama as he turned north at the tiny community of Haast and gave himself over to full enjoyment of the spectacular drive. Gigantic ferns grew alongside the road, mixed with other forms of plant life that were unknown to him. Despite the lack of almost any traffic, he was forced to keep a slow pace to handle the constant twists in the road, the frequent one-way bridges, and the narrow pavement.

When he at last reached Franz Josef, it was rapidly growing dark. Among the few buildings he found a motel, where he checked in. An inviting dining room provided a very acceptable dinner. Before he had finished his meal, it had begun to pour rain.

In the morning the rain was still coming down, with no signs of relenting. As soon as he had finished his breakfast, Peter checked out, got back into his little car and started north. He had driven several hundred feet before he was abruptly reminded that he was driving on the right; he had to swerve sharply to avoid a pedestrian who stood, utterly confused, in the middle of the roadway.

In the still-continuing rain he drove on, taking what pleasure he could from the shifting vistas of the Tasman Sea but concentrating on the highway, which was narrow and much too winding for comfort. Trees overhung the pavement, and rich ferns reached out like parts of a tropical rain forest, while thick underbrush showed that the land was little used. When he reached a fairly long, completely empty stretch of road that was almost straight, he allowed himself the brief luxury of driving on the right-hand side. He drew a deep, comforting breath and lifted his shoulders to ease the muscle strain.

Without warning, his windshield was suddenly filled by a large object falling directly in front of him. In violent reaction he hit the brakes as something substantial smashed hard on the hood. An instant later, the car went into a severe skid. He spun the wheel in an attempt to recover, sickeningly aware that he had been driving dangerously fast on the slick roadway.

When the car at last slid to a stop, he took a few seconds to make sure that he was all right. Then, oblivious to the rain, he got out on shaking legs to see what it was he had hit. A gripping cold fear seized every part of his body.

On the pavement the body of a man was lying face down. His arms were spread wide, his head was turned at a sharp angle, and he lay absolutely still. As Peter bent over him in near panic, he saw that the man's jaw hung loosely open and that he showed no visible signs of life.

CHAPTER 7

Crushing guilt hit Peter like a hammer blow. For a few seconds his mind was numbed by the shock; then a dreadful realization of what he had done engulfed him.

For one shameful moment he considered giving in to his impulse to flee the scene. There were no witnesses, and he could claim total ignorance of the whole thing. Then he thrust that cowardly thought aside and gave his full attention to the man who lay so ominously still on the drenched pavement.

At first look he was middle-aged, substantially built, and dressed in heavy work clothes. Apparently he had taken no precautions against the rain and was soaked to the skin.

Peter had had no first aid training of any kind, but he was desperate to do something. He ran to his car, started it up, and backed cautiously until he was close to the scene of the accident. Leaving the left door open, he took hold of the unconscious man under his arms from behind and dragged him the few feet to the car. Because he was an inert dead weight of two hundred pounds or more, Peter had to summon all of his strength to get the injured man up and into position on the left front seat. Breathing hard, he fastened the shoulder harness to hold the victim in position.

He spent a few more seconds in the streaming rain making sure that nothing had been left on the roadway, then he got behind the wheel. It was a long way back to Franz Josef, and he had seen few facilities there. Greymouth, somewhere ahead, was a city and certainly should have a hospital. His decision made, he put the car into gear and started up carefully on the slippery pavement.

Knowing that time might be essential, he drove as fast as he dared, keeping himself superalert. His full attention was focused on his driving, but he gave an occasional quick glance at his motionless passenger. He kept hoping that the man would stir, that he would lift his head or show any sign at all of vitality.

Time lost its meaning for him as he drove, knowing that the road would eventually take him to his destination. Finally, at the outskirt of a town, he spotted a small corner store marked DAIRY. Without hesitation he pulled up against the right-hand curb and got out as quickly as he could, running the few steps to the store.

A substantial woman behind the counter was sacking some potatoes for a customer. When she looked up in startled surprise, Peter spoke as rapidly as he could with clarity. "I have a man in my car who was badly hurt on the road. He's unconscious. Where can I get help?"

The woman stopped work immediately and came to him. She supplied quick directions to the hospital and then repeated them. "We're a small town, so it isn't far," she said.

Peter hesitated for just a moment. "Should I call there first?"

"I'll do it for you."

Grateful for that, he ran back the few steps to the car and took off as quickly as he could. To his relief the hospital's emergency entrance was clearly marked; he drove up to it with his mind still fixed on the single idea of getting his passenger into the medical facility.

He had barely set the brake when a white-coated man and a well-built woman appeared pushing a gurney. Clearly he was expected. Behind them was the tall, helmeted figure of a policeman.

Peter got out quickly as the attendants came alongside his car. "This man was on the highway," he said. "I brought him here as fast as I could."

He didn't hear what they said in reply, if anything at all, but he was impressed with the efficiency with which they unloaded the injured man and wheeled him inside. As soon as they were gone, he drew a long deep breath and held it a moment, calming himself. Then he was confronted by the policeman. "May I have a word with you, sir?"

"Of course." He had subconsciously been aware that he would have to explain matters to the police, and the sooner it was done, the better. The rain no longer mattered to him.

The policeman was impassive as he stood in his slicker. "Is the accident victim a relative or friend of yours?"

"No, I never saw him before."

"You just found him on the roadway?"

He was seized by the temptation to answer yes and assume the believable role of the Good Samaritan, but he knew it would never work. It was likely there were marks on his car, and the very limited traffic would point strong suspicion toward him in any event.

He drew a careful breath and said what he had to. "No, officer, I hit him."

The policeman, who was also ignoring the rain, held a notebook shielded in his hand. "I see, sir. Very good of you to bring him here so promptly, if I may say so. Since the weather's a bit nasty, would you care to come to the station and give us a statement there?"

That was clearly an order, but it had been nicely put.

"Will you show me the way?"

"Right, sir. I'll have the car around directly, and you can just follow me."

As he got into his own vehicle, Peter felt a rush of relief that his late passenger was no longer shoulder to shoulder with him in the opposite seat. When the police car appeared, he followed it to a small parking lot beside a squat gray building that was conspicuously marked POLICE.

As he parked, he remembered that there had been no witnesses to report on his speed or the fact that he had been on the wrong side of the road. The victim, if he recovered, might testify to it later, but hopefully the matter would be closed before then.

He got out in the still-heavy rain and followed his guide into the police station. When the officer at the desk looked up, Peter noted that he was a sergeant. "Good morning, sir," he said. "I understand you just brought an accident victim into hospital."

"Yes," Peter answered.

"May I have your name, please?"

"Peter Ferguson."

"American?"

"Yes."

The sergeant stepped to the door and spoke to someone out of Peter's range of vision. Then he came back. "Now, sir, please sit down and give me your account."

As Peter settled himself to face the inevitable, he was grateful that his interrogator was such a clearly reasonable, even sympathetic person. In as few words as possible he told his story. He said nothing about his driving speed or his momentary lapse in allowing himself to drive briefly on the right.

"Did I understand you to say that the victim of the accident fell from a height directly onto the bonnet of your car?" the sergeant asked.

"That's the impression I got, Sergeant, but it happened so fast I can't be positive about anything." That was the truth, and Peter strongly hoped that it would be accepted as such.

The constable he had met at the hospital came into the room bearing two thick mugs of tea and a shaker of sugar. Peter took his tea, added a little sugar, and then discovered that he had no way of stirring the mixture. "Thank you very much," he said.

"Most welcome. Sorry we don't have a fancier service."

As the constable finished speaking, a new man came into the room. He was a trim six feet in an immaculate uniform. Peter got to his feet. He could not read the insignia on the uniform, but obviously this was a higher-level officer. The sergeant did the honors. "Mr. Ferguson, this is Inspector Jarvis."

The inspector shook hands briefly. "I hear you had a nasty bit of luck on the road coming in," he said.

Peter was wary that some kind of a trap might be concealed in the way that had been put. "The nasty luck was had by the man I hit," he answered. "Can you tell me how he is?"

The inspector's voice was unruffled. "I'm sorry to say, Mr. Ferguson, that he's dead. However, it's much to your credit that you stopped as you did and rendered assistance."

"Thank you," Peter said, and realized immediately that he would have to add something to that. "I'm very sorry to learn—"

The inspector moved a palm sideways. "I know that you've just given a statement to Sergeant Holcomb, but would you mind repeating it for me?"

Once more Peter recited his story, underlining that his surprise had been total and that he was reporting to the best of his recollection.

The inspector seemed to have a reservation. "Are you pressed for time, Mr. Ferguson?"

"Not pressed, no." Peter was cautious.

"It's quite important that we know exactly where this accident occurred. I'd appreciate it very much if you'd oblige me by pointing out the spot."

"It's quite a ways back down the road," Peter said, and then wished that he hadn't. It sounded too much as if he didn't want to cooperate.

"Yes, I understand that. I'll drive, of course, if you'll just come along."

"Of course," Peter agreed, hoping that would mend things.

"Please understand that I've never seen the road before, and I may have some trouble."

The inspector led the way to the parking lot and indicated a marked police unit. As Peter climbed into the left-hand front seat, he noted two other policemen in raincoats loading equipment into the trunk of a similar vehicle. That unsettled him, because he wanted everything to be as simple as possible. Then he remembered that he had just killed a man, and his whole body tightened. It was not a simple matter, and he would have to watch his step very carefully.

During the trip back, the inspector drove expertly with obvious full familiarity with the road. When he offered no conversation, Peter followed his example and remained silent. He had already concluded that the less he said at that point, the better.

Eventually the inspector rounded another of the seemingly endless curves, and Peter saw a straight stretch ahead of him. "This could be it," he said.

The inspector slowed immediately. "Don't forget, Mr. Ferguson, that a road always looks very different from opposite directions, even if you drive it every day."

"I know," Peter replied. He judged his distances very carefully, then said, "About here."

In response the inspector brought the car to a halt. The rain was still reasonably heavy as Peter opened his door and got out. Behind him the second car was waiting.

He walked down the road a short distance and then turned around. There was a moderately high bank on the east side of the road, just as he had remembered it. He went back to the inspector and reported. "This is about where it happened, I think. I'm sorry I can't be more exact."

When he was back inside the car, the inspector drove on very slowly, carefully scanning both sides of the road. Then he stopped. Peter did not see anything significant, but apparently the inspector did. When the policeman got out, he silently followed.

Almost at once he realized that they were at the exact place where the thing had occurred. As recall flooded him, he began to shake. He could not control it, and his hands betrayed him with visible movement.

The inspector laid a consoling hand on his shoulder. "I quite understand," he said. "Perhaps you will feel better if I tell you that the victim was already dead when he fell onto the bonnet of your car."

CHAPTER 8

Peter tried to grasp that, but it eluded him. "I don't understand," he said.

Jarvis stood with his right hand in his raincoat pocket, looking down at the wet roadway. "The hospital told me that on first opinion the injuries the body sustained when it hit your car were not sufficient to cause death. Also, when you told your story to Sergeant Holcomb, and then to me, you made no mention of an outcry. A man falling like that would certainly scream or possibly yell: it would be an instinctive reaction."

Peter was freshly aware of the rain coming down on his head. "You're right," he said. "I didn't hear anything. But I didn't think of that."

"No one would expect you to. One more point: you didn't run over the man; your car only knocked him aside. That's most unlikely to cause instantaneous death, yet you said twice that from the moment you got out to give assistance, he made no sound or gave any other sign of life."

Up until that moment, Peter had not thought very highly of policemen. To him they were men who gave out traffic tickets and usually failed to catch burglars. Now he faced the fact that Jarvis had made two very sound deductions that he himself had entirely missed.

As the inspector turned the car around, the other two men were taking equipment out of the back of their vehicle. Jarvis waited a few moments while they checked the side of the embankment. When they started climbing up, he seemed satisfied and began to move away.

A huge sense of relief coursed through Peter: by the grace of God he had not killed anyone after all. Freed of that numbing guilt, he was left with the realization that he had had a collision with a corpse. Unpleasant as that was, he could see no reason for him to be detained any longer. Hopefully he would soon be on his way, and no one would be likely to learn of the incident.

"What's my situation now?" he asked.

"Not to worry," Jarvis answered. "We may ask you to remain in Greymouth for a few hours, if you don't mind. If it gets late, we'll book a room for you in the hotel."

That was not what he had hoped to hear, but he would have to make the best of it. Mention of the time made him look at his watch; it was well after two. "What about lunch?" he inquired.

"Yes, we should attend to that. I'll take you to a suitable place."

Peter noticed there was no suggestion that they eat together.

Forty minutes later, he emerged from a restaurant after eating a much larger lunch than he had intended. The rain having let up, he took his time walking back to the police station.

Two officers he had not seen before were manning the day room, but they knew who he was. The man at the desk rose to his feet. "Inspector Jarvis is out, sir, and it's uncertain when he'll be back. He asked if you would be kind enough to check into the hotel just overnight. Your room is already booked, and you won't be billed."

That was not good news, but considering the hour and the weather, he realized that it might be just as well to stay over in Greymouth. "Very well," he said.

He returned to his car and drove through a freshly misting rain to the hotel. He was given an adequate if dated room, where he stretched out on the bed to rest. After all that he had just been through, he could use it.

After dinner, he returned to his room without even a book to read. He went to bed early, hoping for some undisturbed sleep.

He awoke early to find his room cold and depressing. As he

dressed, he consoled himself with the thought that within an hour or two he should be well out of Greymouth and on his way.

He was halfway through an early breakfast when he was told that there was a gentleman in the lobby to see him.

The gentleman in question proved to be a uniformed constable come to escort him back to the police station. Peter excused himself and took a deliberate ten minutes to finish eating, partly because he wanted the food but more to make it clear to any watchers that he was not in custody.

While the constable waited a little longer, he brought down his bag and checked out. His bill had already been paid, including a small bar tab. He loaded his gear into his car and with the constable beside him drove the two blocks back to the police station under a sour overcast.

Sergeant Holcomb was back at his desk; as Peter came in, he stood up. "Good morning," he said. "Inspector Jarvis will be right down." The way he spoke suggested that things were not too bad.

A few seconds later Jarvis came into the room, fresh and immaculate. "The superintendent is here," he said. "If you'll just come with me . . ." He left the phrase unfinished as he turned and led the way to the staircase. On the second floor he walked partway down a short corridor and indicated an office door.

As Peter went inside, a man rose quickly from behind the desk to greet him. The superintendent was slightly under his own height and carried an extra few pounds, but they were well distributed, and the custom-tailored suit he wore disguised them effectively. His face was smooth and clean shaven with a touch of ruddiness that suited him well. The thing that immediately impressed Peter was the agreeable manner in which he came forward; it made things better at once.

"Mr. Ferguson, good morning," he said. "It was most kind of you to stay over to see me." He motioned toward the other side of the office, where there were two semi-comfortable chairs with a small table between them. As he sat down, Peter was grateful that this man apparently understood his predicament and would not be holding him responsible for it. "Terrible thing that happened to you," the superintendent said as soon as they were seated. "It must have given you a very nasty turn indeed. But you kept your head all right: trying to help that poor fellow the best way you could."

The door opened, and a uniformed officer came in with a tea service. It was much better china than had been used downstairs, and the sugar was not caked in the bottom of the bowl. As Peter accepted his cup, he was pleasantly surprised to find that it contained coffee.

"Now," the superintendent said, "I realize what an inconvenience this is for you. I do apologize. However, there's a bit more behind it than may appear, so I do have to lay on an investigation. Since you're already here, I thought it best that we have a little chat before you go on your way."

"I'll tell you anything I can," Peter said.

"Good, very good." The superintendent had some more of his tea. "Just one or two things I'd like to clear up so that we needn't trouble you again—if possible. You're not really accustomed to driving on the left."

"No, I'm not."

"Does it trouble you?"

"Yes, of course it does. Not only staying on what is to me the wrong side of the road, but driving from the right-hand seat. All my judgments about right and left side clearances are thrown off."

"Yes, yes—a good point that," the superintendent agreed. "I have the same trouble in the States. Now, let me make a little guess. You were alone in your car, and there was no other traffic in sight. When you came to that straight stretch where the accident occurred, you allowed yourself for just a bit to drive on the right—sort of worked off the awkward feeling, as it were. Right?"

There was no way Peter could deny that. "Yes," he acknowledged. "It was wide open at the time, and I couldn't see any possible harm."

"I might have done the same thing myself," the superintendent said. "Jarvis did notice that you had been on the right-hand side of the road and in view of what happened, he wondered about it."

"How did he know?" It wasn't a prudent thing to ask, but he couldn't help himself.

The superintendent refilled his cup from the pot. "More coffee, Peter? Oh, I see you're not finished yet. Quite simple, really. The man came off the bank on the east side of the road onto the bonnet of your car. There are some marks that show you described it exactly as it happened. If you'd been on the other side, narrow as the roadway is, it would have been almost impossible, you see. He'd have to have been flung a long way to strike your car ten feet or so farther from the embankment."

Peter drank a little more coffee in silence, then he made a swift decision to take the initiative. "Superintendent, I haven't heard your name."

"Oh, so sorry. Winston, just like Churchill. But that's where the resemblance stops, I fear."

"Nobody has told me anything about the man who fell on my car," Peter continued. "Naturally, I'm concerned."

"Of course you are! And to your credit, too. But we'd rather not say anything about him at the moment."

"By which I take it he wasn't a local man," Peter said easily.

The superintendent gave him a quick, slightly surprised glance. "I did mention that there is more to this than appears. By the way, just what brought you here? We'd like to think it was the beauty of the country. Or are you a keen fisherman?"

"No," Peter answered. "I've never been fishing." He relaxed into an easily accepted story. "Recently I went through a divorce that tore me up quite a bit. I wanted to get away for a while, and New Zealand was recommended. So I came."

The superintendent ignored a telephone that rang once on the desk. "Let me understand, Peter: you came here for a rest. And you had the means to travel on your own."

"That's about it," Peter agreed.

The superintendent finished his cup and then furrowed his brow for a moment. "You know, Peter, I had hoped you might have said something different. It's true you have a tourist visa,

40

but the word we have is that you were sent here by an American construction company strictly on business. This company is under attack by a major conglomerate, specifically Pricane Industries, and you are in New Zealand to try to gain control of a large block of their stock being held in this country. Now, what do you have to say to that?"

CHAPTER 9

For two or three seconds Peter shut his eyes to escape from everything around him. He had been caught so totally off guard, his brain was momentarily numb.

How in hell had he gotten into this mess in the first place? He hadn't killed anyone. He hadn't done anything wrong. He had even been praised for bringing the victim right to the hospital. But he had just blatantly lied to a high-ranking police official, and he had no way of denying it.

The superintendent sat perfectly still, his agreeable cordiality a bitter memory.

Peter knew he had to say something, find some kind of a defense. "Are you acquainted with a Mr. Ray O'Malley, an attorney?" he asked.

The superintendent nodded. "I know him well," he said. "He's a prominent and very respected man."

"Then I assume you've spoken with him recently."

A shade of hardness crept into the superintendent's voice. "As a matter of fact, I haven't. If Mr. O'Malley is engaged in any business dealings with you, he hasn't disclosed them to us. That would be a breach of professional ethics he'd never commit."

"How about a Mr. Bishop?"

"If we're thinking of the same man, forget it."

That exhausted the possibilities in New Zealand. Peter would have sworn that no one else in the country had any knowledge of his mission, but obviously someone did. He made a decision. "I want to get my briefcase," he said. "I'll be right back."

41

"Don't bother; I'll have it fetched." The superintendent moved to the desk and picked up the phone. As he did so, Peter handed over the keys to the superintendent, who spoke briefly and then left the room.

Given a few precious moments in which to think, Peter tried to evaluate his situation. He had only been trying to cover his tracks. There was no way he was going to let Pricane find out where he was, and why.

The only bad thing he faced was the lie he had told, one that business discretion had dictated.

That thought was still in his mind when the superintendent came back into the room carrying his briefcase. He handed it over and sat down once more. In a surprisingly mild voice he asked, "Is there something you want to show me, Peter?"

"Yes. It's a private letter to Mr. Bishop from the head of our company. I hope to hand it to him personally. If not, I'll give it to Mr. O'Malley. It explains our position."

"I understand," the superintendent said. "We're quite used to keeping confidences, in our line of work."

Since it was the only way to get himself out of trouble, Peter took the letter from his briefcase and handed it over.

Winston put on a pair of glasses and began to read. He did so carefully, turning to the second page only after he had absorbed the first. Most of what the letter contained he undoubtedly already knew. How he had found out, Peter had no idea.

When he had finished, the superintendent looked up. "How did you happen to draw this assignment, Peter?"

"Partly because my mother came from New Zealand."

"I find that most interesting. What was her name?"

"Harriet Oldshire, before she was married. I was still very young when she died. Leukemia."

"I'm sorry to hear that. Oldshire, you say—rather an odd name. Do you happen to know what part of the country she came from?"

"The South Island, I think, but I don't know for sure. After she passed away, my father was a different man. He could hardly ever bring himself to speak of her."

"Is he still living?"

"No."

"Brothers or sisters?"

A wave of bitterness touched him, and he yielded to it. "I'm surprised you don't already know that. No, none."

"We didn't check you out that thoroughly, Peter. I saw no need for it. I did happen on the fact that you're divorced. Have you a new lady friend?"

Peter shook his head; it was easier.

The superintendent took off his glasses and tucked them away. "Of course you're not to blame for the incident on the highway. You stopped and rendered assistance when others might have driven away, hoping to escape responsibility. We almost always find them out, but you probably didn't know that."

"No, I didn't."

"Now, Peter, you did a very unwise thing when you gave me an untruthful answer to an important question. I told you that I was going to lay on an investigation. Do you recall that?"

"Yes," Peter acknowledged. "I didn't realize the importance of our conversation. Please accept my apology."

Winston considered that for a moment. "In view of your admission of error, I'll excuse you this time, Peter. And I'll not publish the reason why you're here, even though your visa isn't in order."

That was a great relief for Peter; he was out of the mess at last. But one thing still bothered him. "You told me that this matter was serious, beyond the fact that a man was killed," he said. "Since I seem to be involved in some way, can you tell me any more about it?"

Winston was cautious. "That's a rather delicate question, Peter. Why do you think you're involved?"

"Yesterday, Inspector Jarvis told me that I'd acted properly and that I wasn't responsible for the death of the man who was killed. That should have been enough to clear me right there. But I was still asked to stay here overnight, and now I'm being interviewed again about an incident that wasn't my fault."

It was silent in the room for so long, Peter began to wonder if had just made another serious mistake. It was not his function to inquire into police business. Then Winston raised his head, almost with a jerk.

"What you say is true, Peter; you're involved more than you know. Perhaps it's best you should be warned. But first, let me ask another question: do you intend to do anything beyond seeing Ray O'Malley, and possibly Mr. Bishop, while you're here?"

"I thought I might try to look up my relatives if there are any left. It's probably my only chance."

There was a slight tap on the door, then a constable came in and handed the superintendent an envelope. "A message for Mr. Ferguson," he said, and left.

This time Peter's presence of mind was with him. "Why don't you read it?" he suggested.

"It could be personal."

"I don't know anyone here that well."

The superintendent tore open the envelope and read aloud:

RETURN IMMEDIATELY QUEENSTOWN AND REMAIN THERE PENDING INTERVIEW WITH O'MALLEY. DISTURBED YOUR IN-VOLVEMENT WITH POLICE.

CHARLES

"May I see that?" Peter asked. He took the form, read it carefully twice, and handed it back. "It's a fake," he said.

"Are you sure?"

"Yes. I don't know who sent it or why, but it isn't from my boss."

Superintendent Winston gave him his full attention. "How can you tell?" he asked.

"There's a several hours time difference between here and our home office," Peter answered. "There's no way anyone could have gotten the word about me back there in the middle of the night and sent that cable here so fast."

Winston nodded. "I confess I thought of that too when I read it."

"There are some other points you wouldn't know," Peter continued. "My boss and I are close friends, over and above our business association. He'd never be that abrupt with me, even in telegraph language. Or with anyone else; it simply isn't his style."

"I see," the superintendent said.

Peter wasn't through. "Another thing: he's always Charlie, even to the night watchman. He'd never send me, or anyone else, a wire and sign it Charles."

Winston was impressed. "You have me convinced," he said.

"Then let me put the ball in your court," Peter countered. "If you can find out who sent that wire and why, you may have something."

"Oh, I intend to do that." The superintendent spoke with a fresh briskness in his voice as he picked up the telephone. "Put me through to Wellington," he said.

When he had reached his party, he spoke quite openly. "Winston here. I've been visiting with Mr. Peter Ferguson here in Greymouth. He'll be returning to Queenstown shortly; ask Woodley to arrange his accommodation as before. Mr. Ferguson should arrive sometime later this evening. He'll be driving. Woodley has the number of his car. One moment."

The superintendent covered the mouthpiece and spoke to Peter. "Would you mind taking a passenger with you?"

"I'd be glad of the company."

Winston spoke again in to the telephone. "Sergeant Holcomb will be coming with him."

He hung up and then turned. "Peter, you're free to go, with our official thanks for your help and cooperation. I'm sorry I had to be rough with you, but there's a valid reason. To make up for it in part, I'll tell you that your mother had a sister who's presently living in Te Anau. That's not far from Queenstown. Sergeant Woodley has her name and address."

Peter swallowed hard. "Thank you very much" was all he could think to say.

"Now, since you're obviously capable of keeping a confidence, I'll give you some additional information. You're not to discuss what I'm about to tell you with anyone, barring commissioned police officers—is that agreed?"

"Yes," Peter answered, "absolutely."

"Pricane isn't the only outside agency that's creating difficulties at the moment. Some very undesirable people from Australia have recently come here illegally. They are already causing some serious problems."

"I could be mistaken for one of them," Peter suggested.

"Yes, exactly, which is one reason why we checked up on you. I suggest that for the present you remain in the Queenstown area and perhaps look up your aunt."

Peter rose to his feet and held out his hand. "I hope the dead man was one of those you're after," he said. As soon as he had spoken, he realized how bad that sounded, but he knew that Winston would understand.

For a moment a shadow seemed to pass across the superintendent's smooth features, then he spoke very factually. "I wish that were true also, Peter, but it isn't. He was a police officer."

CHAPTER 10

It was still early evening when Sergeant Holcomb pulled into the parking lot of the Mountaineer Establishment in Queenstown. He had driven the whole distance, despite Peter's offer on several occasions to relieve him.

They were cordially greeted at the desk, where Peter was assigned his old room at his request. After a quick shower and some fresh clothes, he went down to the lobby and straight into the dining room. He did his duty by looking around quickly to see if Holcomb was there, then gratefully took a table by himself.

He was indulging in dessert when a tall young policeman came into the dining room. He looked about in a quiet, businesslike manner. He spotted Peter and approached his table. "Mr. Ferguson?" he asked.

"Yes," Peter answered, indicating the vacant chair at his table. He hoped that in this small community it was clear he wasn't being busted. He was just about to offer the policeman coffee when a waitress set a steaming cup of tea before his guest instead.

Sergeant Woodley produced a notebook. "Mr. Ferguson, we understand that your late mother was a kiwi—a New Zealander, that is."

"That's right, she was."

Woodley consulted his notes. "There was a lady named Harriet Oldshire who was born fifty-nine years ago in Te Anau. According to records on file, she later emigrated to America."

A sudden warm feeling flooded Peter and made him anxious for more information. "I'm sure she was my mother," he said. "Is there anything on file concerning her marriage?"

"No, sir, not here. But our people in Te Anau have located a lady currently living there who is her younger sister."

An almost totally forgotten, deeply buried memory surfaced in Peter's mind. "Martha," he said.

"Yes, sir, that's what I have here. One of our lads spoke to her earlier today. She confirmed that her sister Harriet had married a man named Ferguson, an American."

Peter drew a deep breath. "Sergeant, this means a great deal to me. Can you tell me how to reach her?"

The sergeant consulted his notebook once more. "This lady, who would be your aunt, I believe, is Mrs. Martha Glover." He wrote carefully on a blank page and then tore it out. "Here is her address and telephone number."

"Did you tell her I was here?"

"No, but she may very well have heard. Almost everyone else has."

Peter did not know why he had attracted so much notice, but he had no time to concern himself with that. "How close is Te Anau to here?" he asked.

"Quite close. You could easily drive over in the morning."

As a fresh wave of emotion hit him, Peter rose to his feet. "If you'll excuse me I think I'd like to try calling her right now."

"Good luck," the sergeant said, and picked up his tea cup.

Peter went quickly into the lobby, where he picked up a phone and gave his call to the hotel operator. While he waited, he stood very still, letting his mind find its own path.

A richly accented, mature voice came on the line. "Martha Glover here."

"Good evening, Mrs. Glover. My name is Peter Ferguson, and I believe that I'm your nephew."

"Peter! Then it's true! Where are you?"

"In Queenstown."

"Why, that's close by. How soon are you coming. Tell me quickly."

"Tomorrow, if you'd like. I could drive over in the morning if that's convenient."

"Of course it's convenient! I can't wait."

"I'll try to leave about nine," he said. He added his good-byes and then hung up with a genuinely warm feeling.

In the morning he rose fairly early, had a good breakfast, and then drove to the local police station. Sergeant Woodley was expecting him.

"I spoke with Mr. Winston this morning," he said. "I'm to tell you that Inspector Jarvis has issued a report absolving you from any blame for the highway incident."

"I'm very grateful," Peter responded. "Is there anything new on the subject? Naturally, I'm interested."

"Yes, Mr. Ferguson, but it's a police matter at the moment. Now—" Woodley turned to a desk behind him and picked up a piece of paper—"I've drawn a little map for you."

It had been carefully done to show both the highways to be followed to Te Anau and the location of the house within the small community. "If you get lost when you arrive, anyone will be able to show you where the Glovers live. They're well-known locally."

Peter accepted the map, spoke his thanks, and got back into his car. Minutes later he was out of Queenstown and on the open road. As he drove through the attractive countryside, he was freshly aware that ever since he had come to New Zealand, something had been hanging over him.

He remembered several occasions when his identity had

48

seemed to create some kind of undercurrent. He very much hoped that his aunt, when he met her, would be able to clear it up.

In less than three hours he reached Te Anau, a small community on the shore of a magnificent lake. Two blocks before the water, he found the street he wanted and turned right. He rounded a gentle bend and found a small sign with the right number at last. He turned left up a short driveway and was astonished to find himself on the grounds of an impressive estate. The house was almost a mansion. A little awed, he got out of his car and walked toward the front door.

Before he was halfway there, it was opened by a remarkably attractive woman. As he approached her, he saw that her face was still virtually unwrinkled. It was a face he almost seemed to recognize, one that was burned in his memory. "Good morning," he said. "I'm Peter Ferguson."

"I know," the woman answered. "I can see it in your face. I'd know you anywhere."

He took her offered hands, and electricity flowed into him. "I thought for just a moment—" he began, then stopped when the pressure of her fingers tightened on his.

"Yes, Harriet and I did look alike. Many people thought we were twins. Come in, Peter, please come in!"

She led him through a cool, Spanish-tiled lobby into a large living room. Two men who were waiting there rose to greet him.

"Peter," the lady said, "this is my husband Edmund."

Peter stepped forward and shook hands.

"And our very dear friend, Ray O'Malley."

It took Peter a few moments to recover from that. He shook hands formally while, figuratively, he got his breath back. "I believe we spoke on the phone," he said.

"Yes, we did," O'Malley confirmed.

Peter realized that that topic should be dropped immediately: it was neither the time nor the place to pursue it. Instead, he stepped back and looked again at his sumptuous surroundings. "Until yesterday, I didn't realize that I had a relative anywhere," he said. "Then the police told me about you."

"God bless them for it," his hostess said, and indicated a luxurious sofa. As soon as he sat down, she placed herself only a foot or two from him. "I want you to call me Martha," she began. "Everyone does. I knew I had a nephew; we've been trying to find you. Now tell us about yourself."

At that moment Peter was much embarrassed by O'Malley's presence, but there was nothing he could do about it. He summarized his life history as briefly as he could. When he came to his divorce, he didn't try to make himself blameless.

At that point O'Malley interrupted him. "Excuse me," he said, "but I'd like to ask a question if I may."

"Go ahead."

"If I'm not prying, what kind of a settlement did you arrive at with your former wife?"

"I gave her almost everything we had," Peter answered. "Most of our savings, our townhouse, and the furniture. In return, I got a release from any further obligation."

"You have that in writing?" O'Malley asked.

"Yes."

"Go on, Peter," Martha interjected. She understood that he didn't want to relive that painful chapter anymore.

It didn't take him long to finish. He told them he had come to New Zealand on behalf of his company, about his trip up the West Coast, and what had happened to him there. He added that he had been interviewed twice by the police and then formally absolved of any blame for the incident on the highway. When he was through, he was uncomfortably aware how much he had unburdened himself to people he had just met.

He was relieved when a young Polynesian woman appeared at the doorway. "Lunch is ready," she announced.

"Thank you, Rangi," Martha said, and rose to her feet. Peter followed her into a spacious formal dining room.

"Normally we don't take lunch in here," Martha said. "But it isn't every day that I finally discover my nephew."

"Amen," her husband echoed. "And let me say that I'm just as happy as Martha about this."

50

He sat at the head of the table with Peter on his right and Martha at his left. As Rangi set out bowls of salad, Peter spoke to the attorney. "Mr. O'Malley, do you think I've heard the last of all this?"

O'Malley shook his head as he picked up a fork. "No, I'm afraid you haven't."

Peter looked at him. "That's not very encouraging," he said. "You know I came here to talk to you. With that in mind, if I find that I need an attorney, will you represent me?"

O'Malley pressed his lips together for a second or two. "I think I could do that. It might be well for several reasons. Do you agree, Martha?"

"Definitely," Martha said. She looked at her husband, who nodded his approval.

"One question," O'Malley continued. "I don't doubt your identity for a moment, but if you had to, could you produce a copy of your birth certificate within a reasonable time?"

Peter smiled. "My company advises every employee going abroad to take along a copy of his birth certificate. In case of a lost passport, it makes it much easier to get a new one."

"Then you have it with you."

"It's in my hotel room in Queenstown."

Rangi appeared to say that there was a phone call for Mr. O'Malley.

As soon as the attorney had left the room, Edmund spoke up. "Peter, we invited Ray particularly so that he could meet you."

"You're only being prudent," Peter smiled. "You've never seen me before, and all you have to go on is my unsupported word."

Martha laid her hand on his. "Peter, please—don't talk like that. We asked Ray here for a totally different reason. He'll tell you about it when he comes back."

He did, shortly. "I've just gotten some fresh information," he said as he sat down. "I'll have to go shortly. With your approval, Peter, I'm going to begin acting as your attorney immediately."

"Please do."

"Then I recommend very strongly that you stay here, perhaps for a day or two, visiting your aunt. Martha?"

"By all means," she answered.

"Then it's settled. Peter, I know the manager of the Mountaineer very well—in fact, he's a client of mine. I'll call and advise him not to give out any information as to your whereabouts. There are some things you don't know yet, and it's quite possible you may be in some real personal danger."

CHAPTER 11

While O'Malley went to make another phone call, Peter followed Martha back into the huge living room and once more sat down with her close by. Edmund drew up a chair to make it a closer group. "I want you to know," he began, "that we tried very hard to find you, particularly about two years ago. We never expected that you'd turn up, literally on our doorstep."

"I'm only sorry that I seem to have brought some kind of trouble with me," Peter said.

"You didn't bring us any trouble," Martha reassured him. "But it is fortunate that the best lawyer on the South Island is looking after your interests."

They remained quiet until O'Malley came back into the room. "Peter, I called your hotel and everything is set," he reported. "If anyone asks, you're taking in some tourist attractions. The manager will call here if anything important comes up. Sit tight, and I'll probably see you tomorrow."

"Before you go," Peter said, "I want to ask you an important question."

"What is it?"

"There's something going on, something that concerns me, and everyone in Queenstown appears to know about it but myself. Also, you've told me that I'm in danger, but I haven't the least idea why. Now that you're my lawyer, I want to know the score."

There were a few seconds of tight silence. O'Malley looked at Martha, who in turn looked at her husband. It was Martha who finally took the initiative. "Peter, please tell us what you've noticed. It could be important."

"On the plane coming in to Queenstown, I mentioned my name to the man in the seat next to me, and he very definitely reacted to it. So did a girl, Jenny Holbrook, that I met at the Travelodge. In Greymouth I had a strong feeling that the police knew something they were keeping from me. They sent a sergeant to escort me back to Queenstown, as though they were afraid to let me out of their sight. I'm not paranoid; I'm not imagining these things."

"There's no question of that," O'Malley said. He glanced at his watch. "I'll try to clear some of this up for you very shortly. If you have it with you, I'd like to borrow your passport for the rest of the day."

Peter reached into an inside pocket and handed it over. O'Malley took it, offered a quick handshake, and then left almost abruptly.

Edmund stood up. "How would you like to drive around to see our town?" he asked.

Peter knew he was being stalled, but considering the circumstances he accepted it.

"I'd like it very much."

Five minutes later, he was seated in an elegant small car beside his host. By tacit agreement all other topics were dropped as Glover drove through the clean and attractive streets of the little town, pointing out the places of local interest. When he reached the lake shore and began to drive along it, he described the splendid national park that began on the other side of the water. In the fresh clear air that was tinged with spring warmth, he transmitted to Peter his love for his isolated country and his respect for its great, unspoiled natural beauty.

Later, somewhere in the countryside, they stopped at a pub for some of the rich, dark New Zealand beer. Peter was beginning to like Edmund Glover very much; his new-found relatives were more than he had dared to hope for. Judging by their home, the Glovers had to be very well off, but Edmund didn't give the least indication of that as he talked with the people in the pub.

It was only a short drive back to the luxurious home where Peter found himself installed as a guest. Martha greeted him warmly and guided him into a small, beautifully furnished bar. She served three highballs at a comfortable table where the three of them could sit together.

"Have you heard from Ray?" her husband asked.

"Yes. He's arranged to have Peter's things sent over on the late afternoon plane. They'll be delivered here." She paused a moment and then added. "He wants us to . . . explain things to Peter."

"I agree that we should," Edmund said. "Go ahead."

Martha turned her glass slowly on the table. "Peter, William Oldshire was my father—your grandfather. He came here from England over sixty years ago. He worked hard, managed his affairs well, and built up a considerable holding in land and other assets."

She stopped and looked at Peter, who was sitting with his hands clasped, his elbows on the arms of his chair, listening to her.

"My mother died, as Harriet did, quite early; Dad didn't pass away until a little over two years ago. He always planned to divide his estate equally between his two children—Harriet and me. When Harriet died, he let his will stand, because he knew that Harriet had a son."

A thin film of moisture began to form on Peter's brow. He swallowed hard and waited to hear more.

In a quiet voice Martha continued. "When the will was probated, all we had was your name, Peter Ferguson. That wasn't enough for us to find you, although we did try."

She looked at her husband, who understood and took over. "It was very widely known hereabout that we were looking for a Peter Ferguson—the right Peter Ferguson, that is. It was in all the papers. Because, you see, you've inherited from your grandfather one of the finest stations here on the South Island."

Peter shut his eyes tightly and tried to comprehend what he had just been told. His palms were suddenly very moist.

"So you see why Ray wanted to be sure that your wife, I mean your former wife, no longer has any claim on you," Martha added.

For some moments Peter was almost numb. He had heard what they had said, but he could not believe a word of it. To reassure himself, he asked, "I've inherited a farm?"

"Not a farm, Peter, a station. It's up Lake Wakatipu, not too far from Castle Peak. You can understand now why Ray wanted to meet you. And why everyone in Queenstown was so interested in knowing if you are the missing Peter Ferguson."

A very simple question came to him, and he asked it. "Is anybody there?"

"Yes," Edmund answered. "It's in use right now and turning a good profit. Ray made a deal with a very capable station owner nearby to operate it until you could be located. His name's Jack McHugh. He's a fine fellow, completely trustworthy, and you're going to like him when you meet him."

CHAPTER 12

As he sat in the dining room of the Duke of Marlborough Hotel waiting for his breakfast to be served, Ted Kincaid was in very good humor. He had had an excellent night's sleep, and the day ahead of him promised to be most interesting. He always enjoyed exploring new places, and the little community of Russell had some unusual assets.

Almost as soon as he had arrived in New Zealand, he had hired a private investigative firm to ferret out the address and as much other information about the elusive Mr. Bishop as it could get.

The kit that Lloyd had given him included a full survey of the principal New Zealand tourist attractions and the state of their development. Pricane had commissioned the survey with a strict provision of secrecy. The final report was less than sixty days old.

Kincaid was not a man to waste time. While he had to wait for the necessary information about Bishop, he began work on his other assignment. The survey report had rated the Bay of Islands the best undeveloped tourist attraction in the country. The semitropical climate combined with the spectacular scenery were said to be unbeatable.

After he had finished his breakfast, he dropped two dollars on the table, despite the fact that tipping was severely discouraged, and walked into the lobby. A quite attractive girl who had been waiting got to her feet and approached him. "Mr. Kincaid?"

"Yes."

"You booked with Susie's Tours, I believe."

"That's right."

"I'm Susie."

"Fine," Kincaid said. "Are you set to go?"

"Whenever you're ready."

In response he gestured toward the front door. As always, he seemed a charming man because he never permitted business considerations to interfere with his personal life. In São Paulo he had made some very tough decisions from time to time and then had dismissed them almost at once from his mind. His insulation was so efficient, his overall mood was seldom influenced one way or another. He knew perfectly well that behind his back he was known as "the Smiling Assassin," and didn't mind a bit. In fact, it had helped to keep some of his people on their toes.

He followed his guide as she led the way to a small car she had waiting. By the time she had fitted herself behind the wheel, he had fully evaluated her—a fact that his pleasant smile completely concealed. He found her quite attractive, twenty-eight to thirty years old, well educated, and sexually active.

Before she had driven her car a hundred feet, he knew she could handle the machine well and had had it for some time. Her little business had to be a one- or two-person operation, Russell being a tiny community and the principal resort hotel they had just left boasted a total of only thirty-one guest rooms. Perhaps she had a reserve or two on call in the event of a sudden rush of clients.

"Would you like a half-day tour, Mr. Kincaid," Susie began, "or a comprehensive one?"

"I'd like to see everything," Kincaid answered.

"Then you will, by car this morning and by boat this afternoon. Do you know our fees?"

"It doesn't matter."

Susie smiled. "I don't hear that very often," she admitted. "Here we go."

She turned expertly and took a very narrow road that climbed steeply up the back side of a commanding bluff until she reached a small level parking area at the top, where a flagpole stood.

Kincaid got out and looked around at a breathtaking panorama. A magnificent blending of water and islands reached for miles in every direction, all the way to the horizon. His rich enjoyment of the scene did not interfere with his acute appraisal of the whole general area. The vista alone was worth millions.

"Spectacular," he said.

Susie was pleased. "It is very beautiful, and peaceful, too. A lot of people come here for the fishing."

"Let me guess," Kincaid said. "You're about to tell me the history of the region."

Susie didn't turn a hair. "This is the place to do it, because the flagpole right there is part of it." It took her three minutes to deliver her prepared talk on the Bay of Islands and its colorful background. Kincaid listened, missing nothing, as he continued his visual survey.

During the next hour he was one of the nicest guests Susie had ever had. He seemed to be very interested in everything. When she pulled up in front of the hotel just at noon, she knew she had done her job well and that almost everything she had said had registered. Mr. Kincaid was indeed a remarkable man.

"I'll be back for you at one-thirty," she said. "I'll have the boat ready then." She thought it quite possible he would invite her to lunch, but he excused himself very nicely instead.

Kincaid went to his room and spent several minutes making notes. Susie would have been quite surprised at his flattering comments about her if she had been allowed to read them. She had not given him any of the colorful history or anecdotes that guides all over the world make up as they go along. He planned to put her on the payroll.

Kincaid did miss one point: Susie arranged for a somewhat larger and more comfortable boat than usual. It cost her more, but she had no qualms about adding a small amount to her bill; Mr. Kincaid was the kind of man who liked things to be nice.

She also changed into a pair of pants and a blouse—an outfit suitable for boating that also displayed her figure to much better advantage. She knew that she had a particularly shapely rear and that her slacks fitted her with comfortable snugness. Mr. Kincaid was very agreeable, and she was happy to give him his money's worth. That wasn't her usual practice, but Mr. Kincaid wasn't a usual man.

When he came out of the hotel, she took him down to the pier and quickly went about the business of getting the boat ready for departure. When she started the engine, she noted the proficient way that Kincaid cast off the lines for her. Backing away from the dock with easy skill, she turned the boat about and set it on course, beginning her commentary, pointing out things along the shoreline.

It was on the way back that he spotted a high bluff that marked one of the many headlands. This particular one curved in such a way that from almost any point on its face a magnificent view was presented. Within seconds he had a whole concept in his mind.

A major new hotel at the Bay of Islands could have an extraordinary potential. As soon as that particular piece of land could be secured, it could be built from water level up to the top of the cliff lying along its face. It too would curve through ninety degrees so that every room would have a superb view. At the very top would be the finest of restaurants with dancing and entertainment. A direct entrance would be provided from the top of

58

the cliff. The whole structure would be effectively hidden behind the cliff, yet it could be at least twenty stories tall.

The cost would be substantial, but that was not a consideration with Pricane; the only question would be the profit potential expressed as a percentage of the investment.

"That would be a marvelous place to put a home," he said. He saw that there already was one at the top of the bluff, but she would understand what he meant.

"Yes, that's a very choice spot," Susie agreed. "In fact, there's a little stir about it now."

"What kind of stir?"

"Some people are trying to buy it, from outside New Zealand I hear. There's a rumor that they're from Hong Kong."

The moment she said that, Kincaid realized that the whole water area opened onto the sea, so that coming in or out with small boats, or some not so small, would be an easy matter. Hong Kong could mean a lot of things, even narcotics smuggling. "What do they plan to do?" he asked.

"Some say a new hotel, something spectacular to bring in the big money. We're all against it, of course. We like things here the way they are."

"I can understand that. My company is in the land development business, but we make a big point of fitting the ecology. We would never put up anything that would spoil a lovely place like this."

He had not mentioned his work before, and Susie was curious. "What do you do for the company?" she asked.

He anticipated a little. "I'm the president."

"Oh!"

Kincaid resumed his easy manner. "What's more, as long as I am, there'll be no spoiling of beauty through exploitation."

Kincaid had heard nothing about any Hong Kong interest in New Zealand tourist development; it was worth the whole day just to find that out. Pricane with its immense resources could sandbag any competition, but outside bidders could drive prices up to ruinous levels.

To his knowledge Pricane had never failed to get its way, although there had been some classic battles in the past.

As they docked, he noted with warm approval the rear view of his guide as she climbed out of the boat. When all the lines had been secured and the cockpit closed down, he joined her on the pick. "That was a delightful trip," he said. "Thank you very much."

"I'm glad you enjoyed it," Susie responded. "We aim to please."

"You certainly have. Please join me for a drink at the hotel while we settle up."

He walked her the short distance to the hotel with such an easy style, she completely let down her guard. At the desk he cashed a traveler's check, counted out her fee, and slipped an extra ten dollars into the small pile before he handed it to her. She put it into her purse without looking at it and went with him into the bar.

They had one drink together before Susie excused herself. Kincaid saw her to the door since she was at that moment his guest.

When he returned to the bar, he was ready for another drink on his own. There was one other patron, a stockily built, slightly ruddy man with a smooth face and a visibly open manner. When he and Kincaid were served at the same time, the other man raised his glass. "Cheers," he said.

"Cheers." Kincaid tipped his glass and took a fair share of the contents. "Not bad at all," he said as he put it down.

"A Yank, I take it. Your first visit here?"

Everyone asked that, but Kincaid didn't mind; it was one of the ways the locals sold their country. "Yes, my first, and I'm very glad to be here."

"Thank you, thank you so much!"

"Not at all. My name's Kincaid, Ted Kincaid."

The other man beamed. "Glad to meet you. My name is Winston, just like Churchill, but I'm afraid the resemblance ends there."

CHAPTER 13

While Theodore Kincaid was enjoying his second drink, his mind was sifting facts and ideas with effortless speed. He was not up on construction costs in New Zealand, but he had heard that the country was overunionized and that some substantial proposals had been killed as a consequence. For the Bay of Islands project, costs would be at a peak because he would have to bring in skilled personnel from other parts of the country. Adding these facts together, he could not assume that putting up the hotel would be a routine matter. The essential curved design, while common in the United States and Brazil, might pose a problem in New Zealand, where this type of construction could be unknown.

But the profit potential was dazzling.

The hotel would be called the Bay of Islands and advertised throughout the travel industry as a new and exciting destination. Transportation to and from the facility would not be a problem. One good idea would be a small fleet of sleek amphibious planes that could pick up passengers at Auckland Airport and deposit them right at the hotel's dock.

The more he thought about it, the more he became convinced that he had stumbled onto a gold mine. He would have to take care of the flap, whatever it was, about the land and then move in.

He was about to leave the bar when he noticed that Winston was still there. The man's accent had identified him as a New Zealander. Since he had been openly cordial, he might be a useful source of local information. Kincaid caught his attention and asked, "Are you alone at the moment?"

"Yes, quite alone."

"Care to dine together?"

Winston was clearly pleased to have been asked. "I'd be delighted," he responded. He quickly finished his drink and then made himself available. Together the two men crossed the lobby to the restaurant. There they were seated at a choice window table, a tribute to Kincaid's favorable impression on the staff.

The ideal weather served as an innocuous topic of conversation until an attractive waitress appeared to take their orders. When she left, Winston spoke. "Since you're a visitor here, what do you think of our Bay of Islands? No empty compliments, now—your real reaction to the place."

"I'll be completely honest," Kincaid said, meaning it. "I've seen many beautiful places in the world, but this is unique. I'd be delighted to have a home and live here." While his words flowed easily, he was also thinking very rapidly. "In fact," he added, apparently casually, "I've been toying with the idea of buying a piece of property as a retreat—a change of pace, if you will."

"That's a fine thought," Winston said. "There are some regulations about foreign ownership, but they shouldn't prove too difficult—for a private house, that is."

For a moment or two Kincaid reexamined the remarkable image that had formed in his mind. He would make the hotel his headquarters when he took over the Pricane operations in New Zealand. A luxury suite in such a setting would guarantee abundant feminine company. His sudden silence did not seem to disturb Winston, who was enjoying the view from the window.

When the waitress arrived with the first course, Kincaid saw that he was in for another overgenerous meal. Apparently no one in the whole country had heard of portion control. When the main course was served, he settled down to it with relish.

When he realized that he had been silent for too long a time, he gave his attention to his guest once more. "Sorry," he said. "I was daydreaming about that house."

"I can't blame you," Winston responded. "Would you mind if I asked you a question?"

"No, of course not. Go ahead."

"Then tell me," Winston's voice was gentle and soft. "How well do you know Peter Ferguson?"

To cover himself, Kincaid picked up his napkin and wiped his mouth, hoping that simple action would mask the shock he had just received. During his business career he had had many unpleasant surprises, but nothing surpassed the one he had just experienced. To give himself time, he took a drink of water; when he put the glass down, he tried to keep his face as innocent of expression as he could. He knew very well who Peter Ferguson was, but he would be damned if he would reveal that fact.

"As far as I know," he said very carefully, "I've never met anyone of that name."

He had a sudden urgent desire to know who Winston was. On top of that, he remembered that others were also interested in that particular piece of property—Susie had told him so. Peter Ferguson represented a very successful and highly regarded construction company.

Since Winston somehow knew about him, Kincaid, then he possibly also knew about Pricane. But how?

The hostess interrupted him to say that Mr. Winston was wanted on the telephone. The stocky man excused himself, rose quickly, and left the room.

The unexpected respite gave Kincaid time to think. First off, he examined the possibility that the damnable man had somehow learned that Swarthmore and Stone was soon to be a Pricane subsidiary.

He *had* told Susie that his company was in the land development business, but he had carefully mentioned no name. He quickly probed every angle, and got nowhere.

Looking back, he realized how deftly he had been picked up at the bar. Score one for Winston on that; he was an operator— as smooth as the most expensive girls in São Paulo. If he represented the other people who wanted that piece of land, he was a dangerous opponent.

Swiftly he assessed his own position. He had told Winston that he didn't know Ferguson, which was perfectly true. There was no way Winston could prove any connection between them except through Pricane, and Lloyd would never leak that kind of information. His own confidential documents were in his room, in his security briefcase. No one without the right custom key, or some special equipment, could open it.

After three minutes, Winston came back and sat down with a cheerful apology. "Awfully sorry. Very rude of me, but it couldn't be helped."

Kincaid took the opening. "What is your work?" he asked.

Winston looked mildly surprised. "Not very exciting, I fear. Mostly just dull routine with the police. Reams of paper work."

Kincaid kept the initiative. "I'm not familiar with police ranks here, so I can't guess yours."

"Superintendent. That sounds impressive, but it's a long way from the top—a very long way." He signaled to the waitress and requested that the coffee cups be refilled. "What's your work?"

Kincaid knew that the ball had landed back in his court. "I'm in the land development business, Superintendent Winston."

"Do you have a professional interest in New Zealand?"

"Yes, and for good reason." He resumed his easy manner, and his words came without effort. "We're a very old firm with a solid reputation. Long before ecology became prominent, we established a policy of always building to suit the environment. I'm not saying that we intend to build anything here right now, but if we ever do, it would be a source of local pride—not hostility."

"That's highly commendable, Mr. Kincaid. What are you commonly called?"

"Ted."

"Fine, Ted. My first name is Hubert, but I avoid using it; Winston is really a lot easier."

"Then Winston it is."

"Excellent. Now, Ted, you didn't answer my question about Peter Ferguson."

"I told you, Winston, that I don't know any Peter Ferguson."

The superintendent leaned back and looked a little hurt. "Ted, after showing such fine reasoning powers, I really expected better than that from you. Now let me ask you directly: how long has Peter Ferguson been with Swarthmore and Stone?"

"Offhand, I don't know."

The moment the words were out, Kincaid realized how neatly he had been trapped. He had admitted that he did know of Peter Ferguson, which put the lie to his own denial. He had walked right into it, and Winston had him by the short hair.

"How long have you been a policeman?" he asked, trying to recover the initiative.

"A little over twenty years. Now, Ted, it is a serious thing to be untruthful to a police officer, even in an unofficial conversation. Let me caution you most earnestly not to do it again."

Kincaid pretended to be annoyed. "Frankly, Winston, I don't see the point of all this. I told you that as far as I know I've never met any Peter Ferguson, and you have my word on it."

Winston didn't turn a hair. "I didn't ask you if you'd met him, I asked how well you knew him. I'll concede that when I first asked you, I hadn't identified myself and you had every right to turn me aside. However, your statement of a moment ago that you didn't know any Peter Ferguson wasn't correct."

"You have no basis for a remark like that," Kincaid said.

Winston took a deep breath, held it a moment, and then let it out. "Ted, you're not using those fine reasoning powers you displayed a few moments ago. A most important investigation is going on right now, one that involves considerations I'm sure you know nothing about."

"In that case, why bring me into it."

Winston refused to be sidetracked. "What I would like you to explain, Ted, is why, if you don't know Peter Ferguson, you sent a message to him in Greymouth directing him to return to Queenstown and signed his boss's name to it. That's actually forgery, you know."

He stopped and let the silence settle in.

"You see, I saw a copy of that message, quite legally, and we traced it back to you with no trouble at all."

CHAPTER 14

As Constable Robin Harkness drove his marked patrol unit through the streets of Christchurch, his mind drifted from time to time from the subject of his duty to his pretty young wife, who was six months pregnant. The fact that this kind of thing had been happening since humanity began to populate the earth did not concern him. It was the first time for Alice and himself, and he was gravely aware of his soon-to-be-increased responsibilities.

It was a very quiet evening. He was alone in his car, which was equipped with a blue light on the roof, a compact little radio, and that was all. For a routine patrol in New Zealand, nothing more was required.

As he neared the car-park area in front of the new American-style supermarket, he slowed and turned in. Although the market was not large, it was open extra hours, and four times during the past ten months there had been an incident. None of them had been serious, but he had been told to keep a careful eye on the premises. From the outside he could see no need for his services, but that morning Alice had asked for some canned peaches in heavy syrup.

In the line of duty he got out of his car to walk once through the store. It was not strictly necessary, but it would show the manager that his request for police attention was not being overlooked.

In the corner of the store opposite the check-out register, seventy-six-year-old Mrs. Enid Wilks looked over the tops of the counters, saw the blue helmet coming toward her, and was utterly terrified. She had already slipped a thin package of soup mix into her purse, and she was too far from the display bin to put it back.

She did not doubt for an instant that she had been caught and that the police had arrived to take her into custody. For weeks she had been rationalizing her minor pilfering as an informal profit-sharing arrangement between herself and the store, but that fiction now deserted her, and she was engulfed by a too-late bitter repentance. Clutching her purse tightly with both hands, she silently swore before God that if He would allow her to escape, she would never do it again. She was even willing to pay for the soup packet if she could get it out of her handbag and into her cart on time.

She was fumbling as the policeman walked past her and paused before the canned fruit display. When he picked a can of sliced peaches off the shelf, she knew that he was only doing it so that he could observe her more fully. She was *caught!*

Outside the store a powerfully built man reached into the patrol car, seized the microphone, and with one swift jerk pulled it free of the radio. He dropped it onto the ground and crushed it under the heel of his right shoe. He had seen the young constable go into the store, but it didn't matter: if he tried to get heroic, he would be handled like anyone else.

The big man strode into the store, not caring if his intentions were visible or not. It took him only a second or two to reach the check-out counter; his size and his very manner terrified the girl there long enough to keep her from pressing the silent alarm pedal underneath the register.

He seized her from behind and clamped her head in the crook of his left arm, almost choking off her breath. She had been serving a customer, a woman, who stood momentarily aghast in frozen horror. The bandit swung the girl in front of the register and barked, "Open it!"

Virtually helpless, the girl tried to obey, but her fingers refused to function. The powerful man shook her sharply and then pressed her face downward toward the machine. The girl reached out, pressed two keys, and the drawer sprang open.

In one concerted movement the bandit slammed the girl hard against the wall behind him. There was a sharp crack as her head struck first; her knees unlocked, and she slid to the floor.

Constable Harkness was walking down the rearmost aisle when he sensed an abrupt change in the atmosphere of the store. It was too quiet. Then there was a hard crash, as though someone had taken a severe fall. He began to run to the front of the store as a piercing half-scream was abruptly cut off.

As the register area came into his view a swift burst of new energy filled his body, and although the hold-up man was big, that made no difference to him at all. "Halt!" he yelled, and lunged.

On the check-out counter there were three of the stiff rubber sticks used to mark the spaces between orders. The bandit seized one of them and whipped it through the air. It caught Harkness on the side of his jaw and neck and sank into the flesh with deadly force. Harkness went down; the can of peaches he had been holding in his right hand slipped from his fingers.

The robber paid him no more attention. With swift movements he filled a paper bag with the money in the register. He dumped the coin drawer into it and then grabbed the larger bills that had been out of sight underneath. The woman who had been checking out started to cry for help; with a half-sneer he threw her aside so viciously, she slid almost five feet toward the first of the display counters.

Ignoring the swimming pain in his head, Harkness tried to get to his feet: he was down but not out. The robber grabbed the paper sack of money and vaulted the counter, coming toward Harkness with two swift strides. As he shifted his weight onto his left foot, Harkness knew that a viciously hard, focused kick was coming. He stayed bent over, seized the can of peaches, and flung it with all the force he could muster directly into the bandit's face.

It failed to stop him. The woman shopper who had been thrown to the floor was back on her feet seconds after the robber had run out of the door. She quickly found the telephone behind the counter and dialed the emergency number. As soon as it was answered, she began to tell what had happened.

The officer in the communications room cut her off to ask the exact location. As soon as she gave him the name of the market, he whirled and shouted just loud enough to be heard clearly by the other three men on duty in the room, "Strong-arm robbery; constable down." He gave the location, then went back to the caller.

"We're coming, ma'am," he said. "Please tell me the rest."

The courageous woman was still giving him the details when the first back-up unit arrived at the scene. By the time a doctor arrived at the market, three more constables were on hand. Less than two minutes later, the inspector in command of the shift came to take personal charge. An ambulance was in front of the door, waiting for the doctor's instructions.

The check-out girl was the worst hurt; the doctor was giving her his full attention. Meanwhile the ambulance attendants were doing what they could for Constable Harkness and for the lady who had been thrown to the floor. The inspector took quick statements from the officers on hand. He wanted very much to talk to Harkness, but being a compassionate man, he waited until the doctor could attend him first.

The other witness, a Mrs. Enid Wilks, seemed so upset by the police presence that she was hardly able to talk. Unknown to the inspector, she still had the incriminating packet of soup mix in her purse, and with all of the policemen about, there was no chance at all for her to get rid of it. The constable who tried to take her statement was gentle with her and most considerate, but all he could elicit was a complete denial that she had seen anything at all. Despite her age, the constable refused to believe that, but the more he tried to win her over, the more terrified she seemed to become.

The doctor called the ambulance attendants and had them take the girl clerk away. He had done his best to stabilize her, but he needed some skull X-rays before he could proceed further.

As soon as she had been loaded onto a gurney, he turned to Constable Harkness. There was already a bad swelling on his neck. He sat with his back propped up against the end of a display counter, holding his side in obvious agony. The inspector evaluated his condition and used the land-line telephone to summon another ambulance. It was urgent that Constable Harkness tell what he knew of the robbery, but the doctor waved the policeman away. "He's in too much pain right now," the doctor said as he continued his work.

The customer who had phoned in had no more than a few skin abrasions. She was an out-of-doors type of woman, and a simple thing like being knocked down was not about to daunt her.

She declined medical help and then, at the inspector's urgent request, gave a concise and accurate account of what had happened. In the inspector's eyes she was a pearl of great price—a witness who kept possession of herself, who knew what she had seen, and who was articulate in describing it. He had a firm feeling that when the bandit was captured, she would give evidence in court that would be of great help to the prosecution.

The inspector went out to his car and returned with a large brown envelope imprinted OHMS. He opened it and removed some pictures. He began to lay them out in a row on the counter, but as soon as he put the second one down, his witness stopped him. "That's him!" she declared. "No doubt about it."

The inspector was about to ask her if she was sure, but the question had already been answered. He finished laying out six pictures, mixed them about a bit, and asked Mrs. Wilks to be kind enough to look at them. The slight, elderly woman shut her eyes tightly, trying by that tactic to remove herself from the scene. It was not effective; when she opened them again, nothing had changed and she still had that incriminating packet of soup mix in her purse. She tried to protect herself by simply shaking her head. Then, perhaps, they would let her get away from there.

The reliable witness spoke once more. "Inspector, I'm a teacher, and I'm quite good about people. That is positively the man who was here tonight, though how you got a picture of him so fast I can't even guess."

The inspector believed her because it all fitted. "Would you be willing to come down to the station and give us a formal statement?" he asked.

"Of course, but I'd like to call my husband first. I told him I'd only be a few minutes."

The inspector turned toward his other witness. "We'll need your name and address," he began, then changed his mind. She was not in condition to help at the moment, but away from the scene she might come out of her shell and be more useful. "Take her down to Central," he said. "Have a WPC* look after her a bit. Then she may be able to tell us something more."

He had intended that more or less as a kindness, but when he finished speaking, a constable had to reach out quickly to keep Mrs. Wilks from sinking onto the floor. As he assisted her to her feet, she grabbed tight hold of his lapels. "I'll confess!" she almost shrieked. "Here, I've got it in my purse." Her hands shook violently as she unfastened the clasp.

The inspector was not watching. He was outside making use of his official radio. "A good witness has made a positive identification of the villain. Number two of the photo set I had with me."

That was understood immediately—Edward Riley had surfaced in Christchurch. Where he might be by that time, however, was anyone's guess.

CHAPTER 15

After one of the most intense days of his life, Peter went to bed early, hoping that comforting waves of sleep would wash away some of the stresses that still plagued his mind. He rested better than he had expected with the sensation of floating somewhere out in space, separated from all worldly cares and concerns.

When he awoke, bright sunlight patterned the floor of his bedroom. He swung out of bed and stood at the window for a moment, realizing that both figuratively and literally a new day had come for him. In that mood he washed and dressed, then went downstairs, where Edmund met him. "Morning, Peter," he welcomed. "Breakfast is ready and waiting."

Peter followed his host into a bright and cheerful room, where Martha greeted him with an affectionate hug.

"Now," Edmund said, "after we eat, how would you like to go and see your station?"

* Woman Police Constable

Peter hesitated. "You told me it was up Lake Wakatipu; isn't that quite a way from here?"

"Not in a straight line. I called Alpine Helicopters; they had a machine available, and I booked it. So eat up, and we'll be on our way."

As Peter disposed of his food and two quick cups of coffee, he remembered the townhouse he had once bought. It had stood on someone else's property. Now he was about to see some land that might truly be his own, and the thought itself was exciting.

It did not take long to reach the small airport. When they arrived, the helicopter was ready and waiting. Edmund greeted the pilot and introduced Peter. "This is Mark Richards," he said, and the two men shook hands. That done, the pilot helped his two passengers to board. There was a single wide seat surrounded by a large bubble of Plexiglas; as Peter took his place beside the door and fastened his seat belt, he was impressed by the amazing visibility.

As the helicopter climbed into the sky, the unfolding panoramic view was sensational. The lake appeared to grow in size, and the mountains beyond it revealed fresh peaks hidden behind them. Before long, Peter was able to identify the Remarkables and the small populated area that was Queenstown. Lake Wakatipu unfolded into a long lazy Z that was much larger than he had expected.

Edmund gripped his arm. "Enjoying yourself?" he asked.

"Hell, yes!" Peter shouted back.

Near the upper bend of the lake, the helicopter began to descend. Within a minute a large, spread-out ranch house came into view. There was a sizable lawn in front of it, toward which the machine was headed. The approach continued at a steep angle until the pilot pulled up on the collective and the machine slowed to a gentle sink. For a moment it hung poised over the grass; then it settled down with hardly a sensation of touching the ground.

On direction Peter got out, ducking his head although there was no need for it, and walked forward out from under the rotor.

When he straightened up, he saw the massive figure of Jack McHugh coming toward him.

As the engine of the helicopter coughed into silence, McHugh held out his hand. "Glad to see you again, Peter," he said, and then turned to greet Edmund.

Peter looked at the large and impressive ranch house. "Do I really own this place?" he asked.

"If you're the Peter Ferguson we've been looking for, you do. Come inside—Louise is here, and she has the tea ready."

Peter followed him into a large kitchen, where a table had been set with six places. Louise McHugh was brewing tea; beside her, Jenny Holbrook was putting sandwiches onto an oval platter. When Peter showed his surprise, Jenny gave him a wicked smile. "Louise invited me," she said. "Do you mind?"

"I'm delighted," he answered. The day had suddenly taken on an even brighter aspect. He watched as Louise set out the tea and Jenny put two platters of sandwiches on the table.

Slightly to his embarrassment, Peter was seated at the head of the table. Edmund took the other end.

"Well, now," McHugh began. "When you told me on the plane your name was Peter Ferguson, naturally it hit me. I told Bill Woodley at the police station about it, and he made some inquiries."

When a platter was passed, Peter helped himself to one of the inviting sandwiches. "Forgive me," he said, "if I'm a little stunned. Two days ago I was all alone here. Now, suddenly, I've found my aunt, made some new friends, and apparently inherited a valuable piece of farm property."

"It isn't exactly a farm," McHugh said. "It's a station. After tea I'll show you around a bit."

"I'd like that," Peter told him.

After that, the talk was general while the tea was drunk and the sandwiches put to good use. Then Jack McHugh stood up. "If you're ready, I've got a Jeep waiting."

"Let's go," Peter said.

During the next forty minutes he sat beside Jack, who maneuvered the Jeep expertly over a series of twisting narrow tracks, up and down. Within a short time his sense of direction deserted him. He saw sheep and cattle, fences, much open land, and occasional glimpses of Lake Wakatipu not too far distant, but he couldn't form any clear picture in his mind. When they pulled up behind the ranch house once more, he had seen a great deal and remembered very little.

His mind was full, and he wanted to get some facts straight. For one thing, if his grandfather's estate had been divided equally, then how was it that this farm, or station, was to be his?

Louise invited them to stay for lunch, but he declined. He climbed back into the helicopter next to Edmund, fastened his belt, and then waved his thanks as the main rotor began to build up speed. Seconds later, he was airborne.

During the drive back from the airport he remained largely silent, his mind full. When Edmund pulled into the driveway of the splendid house, Martha came out to meet them. "Did you have a good time?" she asked.

"It was great," Peter answered.

"Come in—lunch is ready. Peter, Ray called. He wants to meet you in Queenstown later this afternoon. You're to bring your things with you. After you see him, please call us and tell us what happened."

He made good time on his return trip to Queenstown and reached the Mountaineer not long after four. At the reception desk he was expected. "Welcome back, Mr. Ferguson," the girl behind the counter said as she handed him his key. "Mr. O'Malley is waiting for you in the bar."

"My luggage is in the car," he said.

"Let me have the keys. I'll have it attended to."

Peter walked into the bar and joined O'Malley, who was occupying a booth for two. "I'm glad you're back," he said. "We need to talk rather urgently. The manager's offered me the use of his office. Get yourself a drink, and we'll go in there."

Armed with a dark beer, Peter followed the attorney into a well-appointed office. O'Malley seated himself behind the desk and opened his briefcase. "To begin with," he said, "I want you to understand that technically I'm still representing your grandfather's estate. I also work for your aunt Martha and now you, if you still want it that way. I don't see any conflict of interest unless you want to contest the settlement of the estate that's already been worked out and approved by the Court."

"Of course not," Peter said.

"Good. I've already spoken with Phil Matthews, the presiding judge. He has agreed to go along with my assessment, and Martha's, that your identity's been established. No one's contesting the estate or your right to share in it."

O'Malley took some papers from his briefcase. "I have some things for you. First, a copy of your late grandfather's will. As I told you, it leaves the estate to be divided between his two daughters, if living: if not, to their spouses or descendents. Since your parents are both dead and you're an only child, your claim is clear. It's fortunate that your former wife no longer has any claim on you. Is there any chance you might go back with her?"

"No," Peter answered. "She's remarried."

"Then that's settled. Now about the estate: when it was probated, the judge approved a division that I'd worked out. Here's a copy of that." O'Malley passed a document across the desk. "I advise you to read it carefully. If you're willing to accept it, fine. If not, you have the right to reopen the matter."

"I'm sure I'll not want to do that," Peter said.

"Here in essence is what was agreed to, with the Court protecting your interest. The estate consisted of considerable funds, the station you saw this morning, some other properties on the South Island, and a portfolio of securities. You'll find a full inventory attached to the agreement.

"The largest single item is the station. It's a major asset and a good source of income. In terms of cash value, it represents slightly more than half the total estate. But Martha and Edmund already have substantial property holdings, and Edmund has other interests. Your aunt, therefore, proposed that it go to you."

"If my grandfather wanted her to have half of his estate," Peter declared, "I'm going to insist that she get it."

"Peter, I hear what you're saying, but Martha told me she was more than satisfied. As you've gathered, Edmund is a very successful man. About the station: Jack McHugh has been running it for you for a percentage of the return. This has worked out well. The income from the station, after all costs were met, has been deposited in a trust account in your name. As soon as the Court gives its approval, I'll have the funds released for your use."

Peter folded his hands carefully together to help focus his thoughts. "I need some advice," he said. "I'm an American. I don't live here, and I don't know the first thing about farming or ranching. It seems logical for me to sell the property and invest the proceeds. Do you agree?"

"Let me defer your question for a moment, Peter, to straighten something else out. It isn't a farm, it's a station, and it's just under forty-one thousand acres."

"Good God!" Peter said.

"With that understood, I'll tell you why I wanted to see you so urgently. Within the last few days some Australians have been to see Jack twice about buying the holding. He told them it wasn't his to sell, but they pushed him pretty hard just the same. They want to convert it to a big development for tourists."

"What did they offer?"

"It didn't come to that, Peter. The point is, Jack didn't care for them at all, and I respect his judgment. They virtually told him that if he didn't convince the owner to sell, he might find himself in trouble."

That caused Peter's temper to flare. Normally he controlled himself well, but this kind of threat was a direct challenge. "Who the hell do they think they are?" he asked.

"I don't like it, either," O'Malley said. "I'd better tell you something else. A lodge owner who didn't want to sell his property to some Australians—possibly the same ones—was burned out a few days later.

"That may have been a coincidence; so far the police haven't been able to prove a connection. But we'd better be prepared. The station is pretty isolated, and there aren't many hands. With

76

that setup, if these are the same Australians, some serious trouble could come any day."

As soon as he was up the next morning, Peter put in a call to Charlie Swathmore. Within seconds he had the head of his company on the line.

"I've got some news for you," he reported.

"Let's have it, Pete—pronto!"

"I haven't reached Bishop yet, but I'm in solid with O'Malley, his attorney."

"I hear he's a good man."

"Damned good. You know my mother came from here."

"Yes, of course."

"She had, or has, a younger sister, my aunt."

"Have you met her?"

"Yes. It was at their house that I met their lawyer, who's now also mine. O'Malley."

Charlie whistled over the line. "Great, if it all works out. Have you talked with O'Malley about Bishop?"

"Not yet, but he's agreed to listen to my pitch before he advises Bishop either way. He's no lover of Pricane, or of the way it does business."

"Sounds good," Swarthmore said.

"I think so. Now, bring me up to date on your end."

"Okay. First of all, Pricane got out a four-color mailing to our stockholders. It's clever as hell. It doesn't promise anything, but it implies that by voting for Pricane, the stockholder may double his money in short order."

"How are we doing?"

"To counter Pricane, we've been calling up the stockholders on the WATS lines and talking to them directly. I've had ten people on the phones, me included, and we're getting results."

"So where do we stand?" Peter asked.

"With what we own ourselves and the proxies we've managed to get, we've blocked Pricane from a direct takeover without Bishop. If they get his proxy, we're sunk. There's a rumor that

Pricane has one of their high-power people in New Zealand after him right now. So get on your horse, Pete. The Board meets in eighteen days."

"Charlie, what happens if Bishop doesn't vote his stock?"

"Pricane wins. They've got more votes right now than we have or can hope to get in time. So carry the ball, Pete, for God's sake."

CHAPTER 16

After talking to Swarthmore, Peter came in for breakfast. He went directly into the dining room without checking for any messages. If anyone was trying to reach him, they could wait.

He chose a table, and when the waitress came, he was pleasant to her. "I'd like some pancakes," he said. "Not too thick, and with some link sausages and coffee. Can you do that for me?"

As she picked up the unused menu, the waitress gave him a warm smile. "Of course, Mr. Ferguson, anything you'd like." She put a slight emphasis on the second-last word, and it gave him a warm glow. Dammit, the New Zealand women were attractive!

Shortly, she returned with syrup and butter for his pancakes and a coffee cup. Close behind her, radiating a ruddy charm, was Superintendent Winston.

"Good morning, Peter," he greeted. "Would you mind if I joined you?"

Peter waved his unexpected guest to the chair opposite him. "What brings you to Queenstown?" he asked.

The superintendent waited while a cup of coffee was poured for him. "To be quite honest, I thought it was time we had another little visit."

"What about?" Peter asked.

Winston picked up his coffee and had a swallow. "Do you know a Theodore Kincaid?" he asked.

"No."

78

"He's a Pricane executive who's here in New Zealand. He sent the message you received in Greymouth."

Peter did not respond to that. Instead, he waited until the waitress returned with his breakfast. She set it in front of him with just enough of a smile to let him know he was favored.

Winston ignored Peter's silence. "You know this is a small and isolated country. In some respects we're unique; for one thing, we may be the only country with a declining population. A few weeks ago a survey team came here and began checking out all of our hotels, tourist attractions, and transportation facilities. Naturally, we took an interest. Before long, we learned that Pricane had hired them. Go ahead and eat your breakfast."

Peter began to butter his pancakes. When he had eaten his first mouthful, Winston continued.

"Right now, we're much concerned about a Chinese syndicate in Hong Kong. It controls huge sums of money that it's very expert in keeping out of sight. Interpol tells us that it's heavily involved in the narcotics traffic. When this organization recently sent some people here, we set up a special task force within the police. I was asked to look after it."

The waitress appeared once more and set a hearty breakfast before the superintendent. As she left, she glanced back at Peter for a moment.

"I think the lady likes you," Winston said.

"I hope so," Peter retorted. "Go on."

Winston did, as he ate. "The Chinese have always had the problem that their own people are too easily identified. Unlike the Japanese, they don't travel much outside their own country. So for any kind of undercover operation, they have to go elsewhere for help."

"Like Australia."

"Yes. The Australians are our good friends and neighbors, but they do have a few very rough types among them. We've had a bit of experience with them from time to time. Now a particular group has turned up here with stolen or high-quality forged passports. We think they're working for the Hong Kong syndicate. They're also showing interest in our tourist industry."

79

The hostess came to the table to tell Peter he had a phone call. He excused himself and went to the lobby.

Ray O'Malley was on the line. "We're to appear before Phil Matthews tomorrow morning at ten at Lumsden to determine if you are a true and proper heir under your grandfather's will. If he rules that you are, there'll be some papers for you to sign in order to take formal possession. Be ready at eight—I'll pick you up."

When he returned to the table, Winston was patiently waiting. "I want to ask a question," Peter said after he sat down. "The man who was thrown onto my car—he was an undercover policeman you had planted to watch them. Is that right?"

Winston was silent for several seconds. "Yes," he said finally. "A very good man, and one of my close friends." Then he jerked his head upward and returned to the present.

"He was dead when I picked him up," Peter said.

"Jarvis told you that."

"Yes, but it was his deduction at the time. How was he killed?"

"A knitting needle, or something like that, thrust into his ear."

"Not too nice a way to go."

"No, I should think not." Winston paused. "Have you figured it out yet?" he asked.

"I think so." Peter began to spread jam on a piece of toast. "It was raining heavily that day. Traffic on the road was very light; I met only two other cars from the time I picked up the body until I reached Greymouth. You just confirmed that the man was murdered. I thought so, but I wanted to be sure."

He bit into the toast and enjoyed its crisp warmth. As soon as he had swallowed, he continued. "Now, although I'm an American and am uncomfortable driving on the left, no one could foresee that I would give in to impulse and drive on the right past that particular point."

"True," Winston agreed.

"Put those two facts together, and the odds of a body accidentally coming down just at the moment I was going past are impossible."

He stopped and ate a bit of sausage. "When I picked the man

up," he continued, "despite the rain, I would have sensed if his body had been cold. He was wet, but he still felt warm. So he could only have been dead a short time."

Winston pursed his lips but remained silent.

"The body was on a fairly high bank. The heavy rain had made the leaves slippery, so the man could have begun to slide at just that moment. Or he could have been climbing about, fallen, hit his head on a rock and died as he slid down toward the roadway. But I can't buy either of those options. The only tenable conclusion is that the body was thrown, or slung, down onto the roadway."

"I'm sorry that Jarvis isn't here," Winston said.

"Now, the body came down right in front of my car—onto it, in fact. Considering its weight, which was close to two hundred by my guess, it would take more than one man to do it. Some of Jarvis's men went up and examined the locale. What did they find?"

Clearly Winston wasn't anxious to answer that, but he needed to keep the conversation going. "There were three of them," he said.

"Are any of them in custody?"

"Not yet."

Peter ate a mouthful without tasting it. "The part of the West Coast I saw is thinly populated with a lot of wooded area. A body left up there might not be found for some time. But it was deliberately thrown down. Therefore, the killers wanted the body to be found. If my car had hit it hard enough, the hole through the eardrum might never have been noticed, not with the probable cause of death so obvious."

"Accept my compliments," Winston said.

Peter ignored that. "Several people knew I was planning the trip. A young lady in Queenstown suggested it."

"Yes, Miss Jenny Holbrook."

"The rental car people knew and some of the staff at the hotel. I stayed overnight at Franz Josef. So it was no secret that I was there."

He waited while the waitress refilled their coffee cups. "Obviously," he went on, "they were waiting for me. They threw the body down so I would hit it."

"I think they intended it to land just ahead of you," Winston said. "Then you would run over it and possibly wreck your car in the process. It's a small, light vehicle. But they were a little slow and actually hit your car instead."

Peter looked at his plate and was surprised at the amount he had eaten. The hum of the dining room surrounded him, reminding him that he was still among the living.

"They had two purposes," he said. "To dispose of your undercover man, and to put me on the spot at the same time."

"Yes," Winston agreed. "They got him by surprise, I'm sure of that. They knew about you and where you stayed at Franz Josef. It's a small place, so we were able to find that out very quickly."

"What are they after?" Peter asked.

Winston took several agonizing seconds to make up his mind. "Peter, I'm going to share a little confidential information. One of the survey people I mentioned got himself into some trouble. A bit too much to drink, a traffic accident, and some property destroyed. We had a little talk."

Peter looked up. "I know your little talks," he said. "You offered to drop the charges in exchange for a copy of his report."

Winston studied him for a moment. "It wasn't exactly that, but when this gentleman found himself in difficulties, I did point out to him that he would have to appear before a judge and state his reasons for being in New Zealand, among other things. He suggested that if I could arrange to spare him that, he'd give me a look at the survey data. Privately, of course."

"Which means you have a copy," Peter said.

Winston ignored the comment. "Mr. Kincaid came to our attention very quickly. When he began to show interest in properties here, we checked on him and learned that until quite recently he headed a major Pricane operation in Brazil. Our American friends also told us that Pricane is trying to swallow your company whole."

Peter listened as he savored a last bite of sausage.

82

"Mr. Kincaid is now up at the Bay of Islands, where he has quite fallen in love with the place. He's been trying to tie up a certain choice site. A local real estate man is acting for him."

"What kind of site?"

"The whole end of a small peninsula—one with a magnificent view."

Peter saw it at once. He sat up straighter in his chair and leaned forward. "He wants to put up a hotel," he said. "We've been fighting Pricane long enough to know how it operates. Once the hotel is built, their travel and tours division will book in hundreds of people on a package deal."

He stopped as he caught the waitress's eye and gestured for more coffee.

"They'll operate the hotel and control all the restaurants and gift shops. They'll conduct a national contest with a week at the hotel for two as the grand prize. Their clothing division will come out with a line of fashions tied in with the hotel as a new world-renowned glamour center. Celebrities will be offered free first-class tickets and a holiday, with a girlfriend thrown in if wanted, in exchange for a few photographs taken at the hotel. As far as possible, all of the merchandise offered in the shops—sporting goods, for example—will come from Pricane divisions."

Winston was clearly impressed. "You certainly understand how they operate," he said.

"Know your enemy," Peter retorted.

The superintendent dropped his voice until Peter could just hear him. "At this moment, Peter, Mr. Kincaid is trying very hard to acquire the right to that piece of property. So are the Hong Kong people. Both parties seem very determined, so maybe we'll be able to smoke out our Australian visitors up there. It could be a big break for us."

"You're telling me all this for a reason," Peter said. "What is it?"

Winston ate a last forkful and then offered his open, much too friendly smile. "Let's wait until after your court appearance for that," he proposed.

CHAPTER 17

Throughout New Zealand, by day and by night, the police kept a constant careful watch for the wanted Australians. Teams of officers called at small hotels and fishing camps where the fugitive men might be holed up. The job was complicated by the hundreds of other Australians who were in the country for entirely legitimate reasons. There were a few instances when innocent people objected to being questioned, but when they were given as much explanation as the police deemed necessary, they were usually willing to cooperate.

Every constable on patrol and all of the supervisory personnel were primed to deal with the situation given the opportunity, but the wanted men seemed to have vanished. There were plenty of places where they could have been hiding out, but most of them were in remote areas where any systematic search was almost impossible. Nothing whatever had surfaced, but the vigil continued, and the careful check of all public transportation facilities was maintained without interruption.

For his appearance in court, Peter chose a dark suit with a white shirt and a solid-color tie. He ate an early breakfast and was ready in the lobby when O'Malley came by to pick him up. He expected some sort of a briefing, but following a short "Good morning," O'Malley had little to say during the drive to Lumsden.

As the now-familiar landscape of the South Island unrolled before him, Peter tried his best to put his mind at rest. His real concern was still to get to Bishop in time, but obviously this was neither the time nor the place to bring up the subject with O'Malley.

His mind came back to the immediate present when he found Martha and Edmund waiting for him at the courthouse. Together they went inside and found places in the quiet courtroom where they could sit and wait.

When Court opened, Judge Matthews appeared. His bearing carried with it the authority of his office. He was most business-like in disposing of two minor matters before he called for the principal case of the morning. O'Malley took his place at the attorney's table. Peter was called and asked to step into the witness box, where he was duly sworn.

Calmly he answered questions concerning the time and place of his birth, the facts concerning his parents, and some details of his childhood. The certified copy of his birth certificate was entered into evidence. Sooner than he had expected, he was allowed to step down.

Martha Glover was next called and sworn as a witness. She answered the few questions about Peter that were put to her.

When she had finished, Judge Matthews formally asked if there were any other persons or claimants who wished to be heard in the matter before the Court. He waited a short interval and then addressed himself to Peter.

"Mr. Ferguson, because of the substantial nature of the properties concerned here, this Court has had some inquiries made in the United States, based on the information you were kind enough to supply. The replies received support your claim to being the only child of the late Harriet Oldshire Ferguson.

"It is therefore our finding that you are her rightful heir. Her estate is released to you together with the funds that have been held in trust. You may take possession of your legacy as soon as the tax obligations have been satisfied."

That was all there was to it. On his way out of the courtroom, Peter was stopped by a young journalist, who asked about his intentions. He told her that he needed time to consider his options and left it at that.

On the way back to Queenstown, Ray O'Malley was in a more relaxed mood. "I presumed it was a foregone conclusion, Peter," he said, "but in law you can never act on such an assumption. Someone might have appeared to contest your position; it's happened before."

Peter wanted to be sure of his ground. "Can anyone appeal now?" he asked.

"No. You can go ahead now and do whatever you like with your share of the estate after the tax obligations are settled. I'll take care of that for you in the next day or two."

"Then I have some questions to ask," Peter said. "I've been doing a lot of thinking. First, can I get permission to stay here for a while?"

"For how long?"

"I don't know. I'm an American citizen and I don't want to be anything else, but as of right now I'd like to consider my options. I'll need your advice for that."

O'Malley swung the car around a bend in the road. "Immigration is a strange thing down here. For instance, there's a list of wanted skills. If someone who has one of those skills applies, he has a good chance of being accepted if he fits the age requirements. But he can't see the list to find out if he's wanted or not—it's secret. All he can do is keep on trying if he doesn't make it the first time."

"Age requirements?" Peter asked.

"Yes, above a certain age, you won't be accepted. Your case is a little different. You're now a landowner here, and you're of New Zealand descent. Shall I apply for permanent residency for you?"

"Yes, unless I'd have to give up my U.S. citizenship."

"No, not under the present regulations."

Peter thought a moment and then decided to go ahead. "I don't want to press you in any way—" he began, when Ray cut him off.

"But you want to get on with the business about Bishop. I understand that. I've spoken with Bishop twice about it. You have an annual meeting coming up shortly, and unless he gives you his support, you are going to be the victims of a hostile takeover."

"Exactly."

"I told you, if you remember, that I'd see you got your inning before he makes a firm decision."

"I remember that very well."

"Good. He was interested first in knowing the outcome of today's hearing. Then he wants to meet you. I'll set it up. In the meantime, there are some other people in the Queenstown area I think you should get to know. So I'd suggest that you stay here and keep yourself available."

"What would you think about my moving to the station for

the time being? I'm running up a big hotel bill for S and S, and this proxy fight has drained a lot of our reserves. Also, the sooner I start learning about the station, the better."

"It's a good idea," O'Malley responded. "In fact, Jack McHugh and I have already talked about it. You'll be close enough that you can come into town at any time."

He had no more to say after that until O'Malley dropped him off at the Mountaineer. Before he had lunch, he called the Mount Cook office and asked for Jenny. He had her on the line a minute later. "You accepted my invitation to dinner," he said. "If possible, I'd like to make it tonight. A celebration."

Jenny hesitated only a moment. "I have something on, but it'll keep."

"Good. When and where shall I collect you?"

"I live out of town with my parents, so let me come to the hotel; it'll be much easier. Say about seven?"

"I'll be in the lobby."

After eating, he walked up the hill to the local library. It had a respectable collection that was skillfully arranged and well maintained. When he made his wants known, he was provided with two recent books and a selection of magazines, all bearing on station operation and management.

As he delved into the material, he found it unexpectedly interesting. He discovered important aspects of station ownership that he had never suspected.

After five o'clock, he walked back to his room where he showered and dressed for his date. At a quarter of seven he went down to the desk and cashed a traveler's check. As he was tucking his wallet away, Jenny came into the lobby. She had on an evening cocktail dress that was gathered in at the waist and flared a little in the skirt. It was a subdued dark brown and black mixture that was unusual and obviously expensive. Her auburn hair reached down almost to her shoulder.

"Jenny," he said, "you look wonderful. Thank you for coming."

"Thank you for asking me." She was almost a different girl. The business veneer was gone, and she had become his lady for the evening.

"You know Queenstown and I don't," he said. "Where would you like to go?"

"Have you been up the gondolas? It's quite nice up there, and the view is something special."

"I'll get the car."

"Let's take mine," she suggested. "It's right outside."

It was only a few blocks to the base of the alpine lift, a steep cableway up a respectable mountain to a chalet perched near the top. As Peter started toward the ticket window, Jenny gently drew him aside. "That isn't necessary," she said.

She guided him toward the starting point, where a young man was waiting to load passengers. "Hello, Freddie," she said.

"Hello, Jenny. Going up?" He held a gondola door invitingly open. Jenny climbed into the small enclosed cab that could hold four people. Peter followed her, and the door was closed.

The car glided out of the station, hung suspended in sudden silence, and then began its steady climb up the face of the mountain. When it slid past a tower, Jenny smiled and rested her hand on his. "Look behind you," she said.

He turned to face a breathtaking panorama. Queenstown was already far below, and the gathering twilight made Wakatipu into an enchanted lake with garlands of lights laid at her feet. When he turned back to his companion, he saw that the chalet had appeared just above them, and on the platform a middle-aged man was waiting to help them off.

A few carpeted steps took them into a large dining room. The hostess greeted Jenny warmly before she showed them to the one remaining window table that displayed a small RESERVED sign. She put down a menu and left them to themselves.

Peter took a long moment to drink in the fantastic view of the lake, the mountains, tiny-appearing Queenstown far below, and overhead a vaulting cloudless sky. It all held an emotional richness he could never have put into words, but the feeling charged his whole being.

He looked at his very attractive companion and asked, "What would you like from the bar?"

"A glass of white wine."

When the cocktail waitress appeared, there was another exchange of greetings. After she had gone, Jenny leaned forward. "Peter, because we have so many tourists here, there are two separate societies: we natives and the visitors. We don't mingle a lot."

"I understand that," he said. "I'm grateful you made me an exception. I went to court today. Now, it seems, I'm a property owner here, and I'm thinking of staying awhile, getting used to things."

"There must be a girl back in the States."

"Not really. My secretary and I got along, against usual company policy, but we were just friends."

"Close friends?"

"Sometimes, for mutual comfort and benefit."

Jenny looked at him over the rim of her wineglass. "If you'd denied that, I don't think I'd have believed you."

The table waitress came and took their order. When they were again alone, Jenny put a question. "How long would you stay here?"

"I don't know. I have my job to think of, and it means a lot to me. But I've found my aunt, and she's wonderful. I've never had any relatives before. Ray O'Malley thinks he can get my visa changed since I'm a landowner here now and I'm of New Zealand descent."

"He's a good lawyer," Jenny said.

"I know."

"He has a son."

"How old?"

"Twenty-seven."

"You know him."

"He's a friend."

"A serious one?"

"Not at the moment."

He steered away from that and kept the conversation general until the food arrived. It was satisfactory if not elegant. The magnificent view was being gradually swallowed up by the oncoming night, but it had already made the meal a full success. By the time the dessert was brought, they had both relaxed enough to feel freer in each other's company.

As they rode back down in one of the small cars, he remembered how similar engagements had ended up—at his place or hers. But not this time. He sensed clearly that Jenny was not inclined toward casual encounters, even though her enforced proximity kept him freshly reminded of her desirability.

He was grateful when they stepped out into the cool evening and he was able to walk with her back to her car in a less charged atmosphere.

Before she unlocked it, she turned to him. "It was nice of you to ask me," she said.

He understood immediately—it was their last moment of privacy before going back to the Mountaineer. Taking his cue, he held her for a moment, then kissed her warmly and fully. "Again?" he asked.

"If you'd like."

To answer that, he kissed her once more and then let her go.

CHAPTER 18

Working out of New Plymouth on the North Island, Constable Fred Fisher was on solitary patrol in the early hours of the evening. As he rolled at a steady, moderate pace in his marked police unit, he was glowing with a powerful inner happiness; he had just been notified of his selection for sergeant. That very good news had recognized the fact that he was deeply dedicated to his job. He had wanted police work to be his career, and now the first big step up the ladder had come.

He knew he was not a brilliant man, but he had a reputation for keeping his head in an emergency, and his physical courage was beyond any question. Those were two solid reasons why he had been chosen for promotion.

Within the past few hours, information had been received about some possibly bent strangers who had been seen south of Te Kuiti on the North Island. Vague as the report was, Fisher considered it important enough to investigate.

Because he regularly patrolled the road he was on, he knew all of the pubs along its length and the licensees who operated them. Pubs were a continuing source of human contact that from time to time developed information of police interest. Therefore Constable Fisher always made brief stops at each one along his route.

At the fifth place he visited he was aware almost at once of two men in the bar who could be of concern to him. He thought that one of the men definitely resembled a photograph that he had carefully studied at the station.

As he always did, he walked through the premises, taking his time and exchanging a word here and there. Not even by an extra glance did he betray any interest in the two men he had spotted as he had come in. When he had finished, he spoke briefly with the landlord and learned that the two men were Australians. They were supposed to be fishermen, but a certain hardness in their manner had been noticed. Otherwise, there was nothing. Fisher thanked him and went outside.

As soon as he was back in his car, he picked up the microphone. After the ritual of calling Central and being recognized, he reported his suspicion. Then he continued on his patrol.

Central was impressed enough to divert another car to meet him. If the constable in the back-up car arrived in time, the two officers would then go into the pub together and check the suspects out. If Fisher's suspicions were confirmed, then both of the men were to be brought in for questioning.

As Fisher heard all that on his radio, he was prepared to follow orders, despite the fact that the suspects were both big brawny men. If the party were to get rough, other patrons in the pub would probably be only too happy to give the police a hand. New Zealanders were not men who shunned action.

A mile past the pub, Fisher pulled over and prepared to wait. Because that sector of the road was sparsely traveled, especially at night, the police were thinly spread, and his back-up could not be expected too soon.

He had been there only a minute or two when a blue Rover passed him and stopped. There was still enough light for him to see two men get out of the car. As they came closer, he was sure who they were. He quickly got out of his unit, but before he could turn back to use his radio, they were upon him.

"We need some directions, Constable," the nearer man said in a full Australian voice.

"Gladly," Fisher answered. "Where do you want to go?"

With his last word, an iron-hard fist slammed into his abdomen, driving much of the wind out of his body. Fisher bent over and used his remaining breath to thrust his hand into his deep pocket to get hold of his small baton.

From behind, a powerful, well-placed kick caught him squarely in the groin. Pain shot through his body like lightning, but he did not go down. He managed to draw his small wooden baton, but he got no further: the man who had moved behind him seized him under the jaw and forced his head back as far as it would go without snapping his neck. His baton was yanked from his fingers; a second later, he heard it whistling through the air just before it crashed onto his skull.

Unconscious, he was pushed back into his own patrol unit. The door was slammed; then the two powerful men rocked it back and forth until, on the fourth swing, it gave way and fell onto its side. Constable Fisher was barely aware of the acrid smell of smoke as it began to fill the interior of his overturned vehicle.

The constable driving the back-up unit was a husky young Maori. He had been on the force only a few months, but he was already well versed in good police habits. When he called Fisher twice on his radio and got no reply, he checked with Central. He was told that Fisher was unaccountably off the air. That was bad, because if he had left his vehicle to investigate on his own, he would have reported his intentions first.

The Maori officer tried once more to raise Fisher. When he got no response, he increased his speed and began checking both sides of the road and every possible turn-off. When he cleared a bend and saw Fisher's car lying on its side, he grabbed his microphone.

"Central," he reported in a quick, precise voice, "a mile south of the pub. A police car overturned."

That was enough—Central would dispatch help at once, with an ambulance that could be called back if it were not needed.

The Maori officer pulled his unit up quickly and jumped out

to see what he could do. The wrecked car had already been burned out, although some small flames were visible. He braced himself and then looked to see if his colleague had been trapped inside. When he saw no evidence of a body, he began to sweep the immediate surrounding area with his flashlight. Some thirty feet from the still-burning car he found Fisher lying on his back, his arms and legs spread out helplessly, the sickening odor of burned flesh surrounding him.

The Maori officer ran to his car and radioed in. "The police unit is burning. Fisher is lying near it, unconscious or dead."

"Help coming," Central advised. "Ambulance and doctor on the way."

"Right," the Maori acknowledged, and clipped his mike. He advanced carefully to where Fisher was lying, making a circular approach so as not to disturb any possible evidence. Dropping to one knee, he felt for a heartbeat. When he detected one, his spirits took a great leap upward; he had been almost sure that his colleague was dead.

He ran back to his radio. "Will here," he reported, discarding all formality. "Fisher is alive, but he's badly burned and unconscious. Hurry that doctor as much as you can."

"The ambulance is copying you," Central advised. "Any evidence as to cause?"

"Yes—no accident." Will's heritage had helped him: his dark brown eyes had seen much that others might not have noted as quickly.

"Fred's car was pushed over by two very large men—at least, they've got big feet. The fire's probably deliberate: there's nothing in the position of the car to suggest that it self-ignited, and Fisher doesn't smoke."

"Stand by," Central instructed, almost sharply. Of all the crimes possible in New Zealand, an attack on a police officer always brought the fastest and most determined response.

By a little after nine in the morning, Peter had brought his bags down to the lobby and checked out of the Mountaineer. He was in the restaurant, finishing off his second cup of coffee, when Louise McHugh came in and found him.

93

"Sit down," he invited, and motioned to the waitress to bring a menu.

"I've had breakfast," Louise said. "The car's ready when you are." She was dressed in a pair of no-nonsense blue jeans and a plain white blouse, but even that garb could not camouflage the trim lines of her figure. He wondered how he had missed it before. Perhaps his appreciation of the finer things of life was being honed to a sharper edge now.

He finished the rest of his coffee and got to his feet. "Then let's go," he said.

The car was the same one that had brought him in from the airport. As he swung one of his bags into the trunk, Louise picked up the other and with an easy motion deposited it on top. "I can do that," Peter said.

Louise brushed her hair back with one hand. "I'm a station girl," she retorted. "I've learned to do things for myself. You don't have to hold doors open for me."

Taking her at her word, Peter got into the car on the left-hand side and settled himself down. Moments later, they were passing through Queenstown toward the end of the lake. The vehicle was a moderately old one, but it ran very well, giving evidence of good maintenance.

It took close to an hour and a half to reach the property that was now his. When Louise pulled up in front of the big rambling ranch house, a lanky sunburned man in work clothes came out to take the bags. Peter would have preferred to do that himself, but he had sense enough to accept the arrangements that had been made for him.

"You're in the front room on the first floor," Louise told him. "I'll show you."

She led the way up a wide wooden staircase rich with the patina of many years of use. After a few steps down a spacious hallway she walked into a very large corner room filled with light and fresh air. She turned and looked at him. "It's the best we've got," she said. "William Oldshire had it built just the way he liked.

"The house has been modernized," she continued. "There's a bathroom right there with everything you'll need. Dad's also put in smoke detectors and a fire control system. It cost a lot, but out here we're not close to any fire stations; we have to take care of ourselves."

"Of course," Peter said. He walked over and looked out the window, as he had looked out of windows all of his life. But this time it was magically different. What he was seeing was not just a view, but his own property, land that was his, that belonged to him.

He looked down at his shoes, which still showed evidence of a shine. "I need to buy some different clothes," he said.

Louise agreed. "There's a general store where we get almost everything we need," she told him. "It's only about ten minutes away."

"Can you spare the time to take me?"

She smiled, grateful she hadn't been taken for granted. "Right now?" she asked.

"Any reason why not?"

"None at all. Let's go."

The store was in a plain metal building, but it was surprisingly large and well stocked. He wandered up and down the aisles, with Louise at his side, taking it all in. In less than fifteen minutes, she helped him choose what almost amounted to a new wardrobe. She insisted that he also get a hat. "Out in the open you'll need it," she told him. "All the men wear one."

He took his purchase up front and waited there while Louise collected some other things that were needed at the station. When she returned, she introduced Peter to the store owner, a heavy-set bearded man who wore suspenders and a pair of steel-rimmed glasses. "Mike, this is Peter Ferguson, the owner of Oldshire Station," she said. "Peter, Mike Mulvanney."

Mulvanney held out a huge, work-reddened hand and gave a cordial shake. "Know about you, of course," he acknowledged. "Glad they found you after all these years. Jack McHugh spoke well of you, that's more than enough around here."

"Do you take traveler's checks?" Peter asked.

Mulvanney gave a sweep of his powerful forearm. "We bill the station once a month. Just come in anytime and take what you need. Have a cold beer with us before you go."

There was no refusing that. When it was tendered, Peter drank the cold, dark brew and enjoyed every drop. He had barely finished his can before Louise set down hers, also empty. "Another?" Mulvanney asked.

Peter shook his head. "I've got work to do," he said.

It was the best thing he could have said. With the rear of the car liberally loaded with fresh purchases, Louise drove back to the station. There a woman he had not seen before, an amply built Maori, was preparing lunch.

Peter went up to his room, had a quick shower, and dressed in some of his new clothes. He chose a pair of dark brown twill trousers and a patterned beige shirt to go with one of the two pairs of shoes he had bought. When he went downstairs, Jack McHugh was waiting for him.

The older man approved immediately. "You couldn't have done better," he said.

"Louise helped me out."

"I expect she would, if you asked her. Peter, while you were gone your lawyer called. He left his number and wants you to call him."

Peter went to the phone and got through to O'Malley very quickly.

"I have some information for you concerning your application for permanent residency," O'Malley said.

"Good or bad?"

"You came in on a visitor's visa when it was a business trip, and they took a dim view of that. But when I explained the circumstances and certain other matters, they agreed to grant you a permanent resident visa."

"That's very good news," Peter said.

"Now, Peter, since you've taken over your station, some of the important local people around here would like to meet you. Are you free for dinner this evening?"

"Yes, of course."

"Then meet me at the Mountaineer at five-thirty."

As he drove back to Queenstown in plenty of time for his appointment, Peter's mind was churning; so much had happened in so short a time. But tonight the chips would be down. He only hoped and prayed that when he came face to face with Bishop, he wouldn't let Charlie Swarthmore and the rest of his company down.

CHAPTER 19

As he drove into Queenstown, Peter tried hard to convince himself that he was dressed appropriately to meet the man in whose hands the future of his company, and his own, largely rested. He had accepted that owning a station was going to make a major change in his life, but he had many friends at Swarthmore and Stone, especially Charlie, and he had no intention of abandoning them in midstream.

He had O'Malley's specific assurance that ranch wear was not only right but expected. He could see the sense of that, especially if everyone else showed up that way and he wore coat and tie: that would set him apart immediately.

He was relieved when he reached the Mountaineer and found O'Malley in an open-neck shirt and a pair of twill pants held up by a Western-style belt. As soon as the lawyer was in the car with him, he felt considerably better.

O'Malley drove, weaving his way out of town on some rather narrow but well-paved roads. "I want to tell you a little bit about your host tonight," he began when they were well on their way. "He's a very down-to-earth sort, the kind of man who takes it as it comes and never tries to make an impression. He doesn't need to. For one thing, he's one of the principal stockholders in Mount Cook Airlines and sits on the board."

"What's his name?" Peter asked quickly.

"Colin Emerson. He recently developed a major ski center right up there." He pointed to a sizable mountain slope where two or three lifts were visible.

O'Malley continued, "A while ago he bought a piece of property, several acres of it, that would make an ideal estate. It even has a couple of waterfalls on it. Then he picked the spot he wanted and built his house. By that I mean he built it with his own hands, all to his own plans. It's quite a showplace. I believe he did call in a paperhanger at the finish, or someone like that, but he accomplished what many men only dream of doing."

"I can't help comparing that with the station I just walked in and took over," Peter said. "The house has a wonderful lived-in feeling."

O'Malley drove on in silence for another ten minutes, then he pointed. "There it is," he said.

The house was large and comfortable looking without being pretentious. Peter could see that it said a lot about the man who had built it.

A white gravel driveway took them to the door. Waiting for them was a man of medium build and almost neutral features. His body was trim, showing that he kept himself in condition. He might have been fifty; it was hard for Peter to tell. He was principally aware of the man's easy relaxed manner, which had its own certain dignity.

"Evening, Ray," Emerson said, and turned to his other guest. "You're Peter Ferguson," he confirmed.

"Yes," Peter said.

"Colin Emerson. Come in and meet the others. We'll have dinner in a few minutes."

There were a half-dozen men congregated in the substantial living room, all with glasses in their hands. Emerson stepped behind the bar, built a drink for O'Malley, and handed it to him without asking what he wanted. Then he looked at Peter and raised his eyebrows.

"Something that's popular in New Zealand," Peter said.

Emerson mixed a drink and handed it over. Peter tried it and liked it at once. Then he was introduced to the others. Last names were given once; and after that it was first names only. A man named Tex was introduced as the chief pilot for Mount Cook Airlines, but he looked more like a cowboy than a professional airline pilot; this could have been the source of his nickname. But to Peter's crushing disappointment, there was no Alfred Bishop among them. He had been so sure that he was about to meet him at last.

Shortly thereafter a woman appeared and announced that dinner was ready. The men filed into the dining room and took their places around the table. Emerson motioned for Peter to sit next to him. As he took his chair, Peter checked quickly that all the places were filled. They were. That destroyed his last hope that Bishop might yet be coming.

As he had expected, during the meal Peter had to answer a good many questions. In an apparently casual way they asked for his views on New Zealand as a country and on his station and how he was getting along with Jack McHugh. They asked a lot about various current situations in the United States.

Peter answered as freely as he could, aware that the food in front of him was not fancy, but delicious. Gradually he relaxed, matching his mood to the others. He even ventured to ask some questions of his own.

Finally, his host asked the key question, which he had been anticipating and dreading at the same time. "You haven't told us what brought you to New Zealand. Had you heard of your inheritance?"

Peter shook his head. "That came right out of the blue," he answered. "I'm still trying to adjust to it. I'm not used to being a property owner. I had a little townhouse once, but the land it stood on belonged to a conglomerate. My contact with the management was a computer that mailed me bills with unfailing regularity."

"You didn't tell us why you came," Emerson reminded him.

There was no point in trying to hold anything back from this bunch. "I work for an architectural firm, Swarthmore and Stone. A conglomerate, Pricane Industries, is trying through a hostile raid to take us over. We're fighting it with all we have, despite Pricane's enormous resources. One of our major stockholders lives in New Zealand. If he's willing to give us his proxy, then we'll have enough votes to stop Pricane. We don't want to be bought out by anyone."

"And if you don't win, what will you do?" Emerson asked.

"I don't know yet," Peter said, "because we don't think in terms of losing. Take a nucleus of our best people, perhaps, and start up again under another name."

"Can you do that without breaking your contracts?"

"Most of us don't have contracts; we don't need them."

"Are you a stockholder?" It seemed as though everyone at the table were taking part in his examination. But it was all on a friendly basis, a case of getting to know someone new in the community.

"In a small way, yes." He had already decided not to mention Bishop's name if he could avoid it. He assumed that several of those present knew Bishop and were sizing him up for that man's benefit.

After the meal it was different. As darkness fell, the conversation in the big living room became general, and Peter was no longer the center of attention. After another round of drinks, the party began to break up. Together with O'Malley, Peter took his leave of Emerson at the door.

When they were back in the car and well started on the road to Queenstown, Peter spoke. "I certainly enjoyed that."

"Glad you did. They're good people, all of them."

"I hope I get to know them better."

"You will."

O'Malley seemed so quiet, Peter wondered if in some way he had pulled a gaffe without knowing it. There were different customs here, and certain words had different meanings. He was on the point of asking when he decided not to; if anything was seriously wrong, O'Malley would let him know. Instead, he asked a different question. "Is it the custom in New Zealand, in a party like that one, to say grace before eating?"

"No," O'Malley answered. "But Colin usually does. Because he wants to." He paused. "That's why we call him Bishop," he concluded.

CHAPTER 20

When they pulled up in front of the Mountaineer, O'Malley broke what had been a considerable silence. "I suggest that you stay here tonight," he said. "The hotel can fix you up with an overnight kit. We have a date to have coffee tomorrow morning at the Travelodge with Bishop at ten. Any reason why you can't make it?"

"None." Peter was quick to agree. "Tomorrow at ten." He fully realized how crucial this talk was likely to be; he would have to be at his very best.

"Good. Ask for me at the desk."

In the morning Peter walked the short distance to the Travelodge, asked at the desk for O'Malley, and was directed to a private dining room on the second floor.

Although he was eight minutes early, both O'Malley and Colin Emerson were already there. A small coffee urn was in place, and a plate of tempting-looking Danish had been set out.

When the men had served themselves, they sat down together in a comfortable grouping.

"I've known since you arrived here that you wanted to see me, and why," Emerson began. "I haven't been trying to keep you dangling, but I had to get certain information before we could talk about Pricane and my stock position in Swarthmore and Stone. I invited you to my home last night so that we might meet without business intruding."

"I enjoyed it very much," Peter said.

"Good," Emerson continued. "You might as well call me Bishop, because everyone does. I carry some of the things in my portfolio under the name Alfred Bishop to protect my privacy. Everything having to do with overseas investments is filtered through Ray, who's shielded me from all kinds of unwanted pressures."

Peter kept still.

"Now, Peter, are you aware how much Pricane has offered me for my stock in your company?"

"No, sir," Peter answered.

"Cut out the bullshit—you don't have to "sir" me. For your information, they've offered me eighty dollars a share, which is well above the current market, and that's for openers. They have a man here who's been in touch with Ray. His name's Kincaid. He advanced the offer and hinted at the same time that they'd go higher if they have to. Can you match that?"

Peter knew the answer to that at once: after all of the purchases that Swarthmore and Stone had already made of their own stock, there was no way they could raise that kind of money. "My first answer has to be no," he said, "Because we don't have anything like that in the till. We've extended ourselves almost to the limit buying up every share we could. But let me ask you this: if we *could* match it, would you then be willing to let us be the buyers?"

Bishop shifted in his chair. "I get all the usual corporate reports," he said. "So I know pretty well where you stand. Kincaid also suggested letting me keep my stock if I would sell him my proxy."

Peter said with a new positiveness in his voice, "Frankly, I've never heard of buying and selling proxies. If it comes to matching dollars with Pricane, we're out of the ball game. But if you stay with us, you'll hold a strong position in a damned good company and one you can be proud of. In fact, we have some significant contracts pending for new projects here in New Zealand."

"I wonder how that came about," Bishop said.

"You know we specialize in building to fit the ecology," Peter added.

"Of course. That's why I bought into S & S in the first place. That and your sound management, plus your track record."

Peter knew it was time to ask the direct question. "Will you give us a chance?" he asked. Then an inspiration hit him. "If we're short, I'll put up a mortgage on my station until we can buy it back."

Bishop shook his head. "I'm not that hard up for dollars, Peter. But I've got a counterproposition for you. The Honorable Warren Cooper, one of the cabinet ministers, is going to be here in Queenstown shortly. He had suggested that I set up an appointment for the three of us to meet with him. There is something pending where he feels you might be able to help us. It may take quite a bit of your time. But if you accept whatever assignment he may offer to you, then I'll go along and give you my proxy if by doing so it will save your company."

"And yours," Peter was quick to add.

"Good point. Is it a deal?"

Peter could hardly contain himself. "I don't know what the hell he wants, but he's got it," he said.

At the end of four days Peter was beginning to feel almost at home at his station. He had been over the terrain in detail with Jack McHugh and learned how each section of the property was being used and what was planned for it in the future. The first two days of his orientation were by Jeep, which was a convenient means of travel although bone-jarring at times.

On the third day he came down to breakfast to discover that Jack had returned to his own station. In his place Louise had come over to continue what her father had started. She was dressed in a well-worn pair of jeans, what was essentially a work shirt, and a large hat that hung down over her back. She had her hair fastened up in some manner on the top of her head with no pretense of artifice, but a casual look told Peter that she had sacrificed none of her femininity. The way she walked across the large kitchen toward the breakfast table reinforced his opinion.

She had had her breakfast, but she took a cup of tea while he ate. "Dad told me where you've already been," she said. "Are you beginning to get more of an idea of the station?"

"Yes," Peter answered. "It's enormous. But I've learned most of the tracks now and where they go."

"Good. Dad wants me to take you to some other places around the station, if that's okay with you."

"You know it is," Peter told her. "Without you and your father, I'd be hopelessly over my head here."

Louise didn't respond to that; instead, she remained silent until Peter had finished. Then she led the way out the front door. The familiar kidney-crushing Jeep was not there. Instead, a tall, lean hand whose name was Andy was standing by with a pair of saddle horses. Louise put on her hat, walked over to one of the mounts, and vaulted up into the saddle with a seeming minimum of effort. She picked up the reins and waited for Peter, composed and at ease.

"I've hardly ever been on a horse," Peter confessed. "I never had much opportunity."

"Then we won't ride for too long today," Louise said. "I'll lead and take it easy. You've a gentle mount there, so don't worry."

Peter put his foot into the stirrup, got into the saddle, and settled himself.

Without comment, Louise drew her mount alongside his, and they started off together. After only a short distance she turned off the established dirt track and started across an open field. She rode at a slow and even pace, both horses walking easily through the cropped grass. By now Peter knew they were headed eastward toward a section of the station that he had never seen.

At the end of an hour, Louise led the way out toward the edge of a considerable hill, where she reined up. As soon as he managed to pull up beside her, he saw that the promontory commanded a magnificent view of Lake Wakatipu for miles in both directions.

Louise patted her mount on the side of the neck before she spoke. "There are three places on the station that have views like this. I think that's why some people have been trying to buy it. Dad sounded them out. They didn't say a lot, but he doesn't miss much. He thinks they want to put up a big hotel or perhaps a bunch of rental condos here and then run a dude ranch. They did talk about 'tourist attractions,' as though they intended to turn at least part of the station into an amusement park."

"Never," Peter said.

"Dad told them that the property wasn't for sale, that it was being held in trust, but they persisted." She turned in her saddle and looked him squarely in the face. "You do mean it when you say 'never,' don't you?" she asked.

"I mean it," Peter responded. "Unless your father advises me otherwise, this place isn't for sale."

Louise gave him a grateful look. "Stick to that," she said. Then she picked up her reins once more and turned her mount around, headed back to the ranch house.

Just before five he received a call from Ray O'Malley, who was pithy and to the point. "Warren Cooper is going to be in Queenstown tomorrow and would like to meet with you. He has suggested drinks at four at the Travelodge."

"Precisely who is he?" Peter asked.

"Mr. Cooper is the minister for foreign affairs. In your language that would be secretary of state. A little while back he was

minister of tourism, and he's kept up a keen interest in the industry."

"I'll be there. Coat and tie?"

"In this case, yes. I'll meet you there, along with Bishop. The
minister is a very agreeable gentleman and usually quite relaxed
in his manner."

"You know him, then."

"Yes, quite well, actually. I'm sure you two will get along."

"Ray, why does he want to see me?"

"Suppose you wait and let him tell you that. I'll see you tomorrow." He hung up.

For a moment or two Peter was irritated that his own attorney
had not answered a reasonable question. Then he decided that
O'Malley knew what he was doing and left it at that.

At ten minutes to four he entered the lobby of the Travelodge
and asked at the desk for Minister Cooper. He was directed to a private suite on the second floor. He went up and tapped on the door.

It was opened almost immediately by Ray O'Malley, who ush-
ered him inside. Minister Cooper was a pleasant, rather tall
man, perhaps in his early fifties, who was wearing a beautifully
cut lounge suit. Bishop was there, and also present, beaming af-
fably, was Superintendent Winston.

A discreet waiter came in to take the drink orders. Peter asked
for a martini, while the others chose whiskey and soda.

"Tell me, Mr. Ferguson," the minister began. "How do you
like your station? I understand that you're living there now."

"It's a totally new experience," Peter answered, "but I like it
very much."

Within a minute or two the waiter was back. He served everyone, set down two or three plates of light snacks, and then left.

"May I call you Peter?" the minister asked.

"Please do, sir."

"Peter, I know that you're aware of some problems we've been
having recently concerning our tourist industry. Superintendent
Winston told you, I believe, that Pricane is interested in a certain
piece of land at Russell."

"That's right," Peter acknowledged.

"As soon as he did that, you gave him some detailed and valuable information based on your knowledge of Pricane and its methods."

Peter sipped his drink and continued to listen.

"That was much appreciated. Now let me state the case clearly. We're most concerned with corporate raids being made against our tourist industry. Pricane has a buying team coming into Auckland this weekend. Also, a Hong Kong investment group has taken a keen interest in us. We're having some serious police problems that may be associated with them."

"Very serious," Winston contributed.

"In this situation we believe, Peter, that you might be of some real help to us, if you're so disposed."

"What would you like me to do?"

Cooper consulted his drink before he answered that.

"You're an obvious American who's generally known to have come into a considerable inheritance. It's quite logical, therefore, that you might choose to travel the country a bit, enjoying yourself as a sightseeing tourist."

"Of course," Peter agreed.

"We believe that you're in a unique position to evaluate whatever moves Pricane may make; you've already demonstrated that. What would you say to visiting some of our principal tourist attractions as a government guest?"

"To try and foresee what Pricane might do?" Peter asked.

"Yes, precisely. Or perhaps to be on hand to advise us if they attempt any major takeovers."

"I'll be glad to," Peter said.

"It's done, then," Cooper said. "You can work out the details with Superintendent Winston."

The minister rose to his feet and once more held out his hand.

Winston followed Peter out the door. "I'll be in touch with you very shortly," he said. "Meanwhile, there is something I think you should know. From information received, we're aware that the piece of property in Russell isn't the only one that these outsiders are anxious to acquire."

"I know—they're after any good tourist facilities they can get."

"Exactly right, Peter, but there's more. We happen to know that they're also very anxious to take over your station."

CHAPTER 21

With a reassuring awareness that he knew exactly what he was about, Theodore Kincaid prepared himself for the business of the evening. He knew better than to wear a formal business suit. Instead, he put on casual clothing and planned to walk to his destination. It was a fine evening, warm and balmy at the Bay of Islands, and he had only a short distance to go.

As he set out from the Duke of Marlborough, he was inwardly smiling. The morning flight from Los Angeles would bring in a full Pricane acquisition team to work under his direction. By the time he met with its members for dinner, he would have some very specific instructions to give. He had been carefully busy during his stay, and his plans were well advanced.

While he climbed steadily up the narrow road, he reviewed each step he proposed to take and made sure that he had all of the bases covered. After he completed his errand, he had a date to drop by Susie's place "for a cup of tea." Tea to him was a mild form of poison, but Susie was an altogether different matter. On the one occasion he had been in bed with her, she had been sensational.

A less-than-fifteen-minute walk, which included some fairly stiff climbing, brought him to the top of the site he had chosen. He knew that most of the property was under option to a Hong Kong-based organization, but that didn't trouble him. If his errand worked out as planned, he would end up with a hole card that would be unbeatable.

At the very top of the bluff, on a level spot that reached to the rim of the cliff, there was a small spread of well-maintained lawn and a modest cottage. Kincaid knew a lot about the resident owner and his wife; he had even managed to get a good run-down on their finances. He never willingly left anything to chance.

He knocked on the door and waited. He had no appointment; to have made one could have been a serious mistake.

The man who opened the door was in his prime sixties. He was of chunky build, with hands that spoke of much manual labor and features that reflected an almost fierce independence. Yet there was a certain warmth about him as he viewed the stranger on his doorstep. "Evening," he said.

Kincaid matched his voice and manner to the man he had come to see. "Mr. MacTavish, I'm Ted Kincaid. Could you spare me a few minutes?" There was nothing of the salesman about him; it was the way a friend would speak.

"I don't want to sell my property," MacTavish said.

"I know that," Kincaid replied. "I've got something else to talk about."

"Then come in."

When he had stepped through the doorway into the small living room, Kincaid took one quick look and wished for just a second or two that he could retire to such a place. There was a good-sized window that gave a spectacular view of the water and the islands that were scattered for miles in every visible direction. Kincaid knew that the Royal Suite, located at almost the place where he was standing, would bring a minimum of a thousand a day.

A plain but pleasant woman came in and asked Kincaid if he would like some tea. "Yes, if you're having some," he answered.

She looked at her husband, who answered with a slow nod.

"Sit down," MacTavish said, "and tell me what you're offering."

Because there was no use in trying to "approach" MacTavish, Kincaid came right to the point. "There are some people who want to build a big hotel here. I'd just as soon that they didn't."

MacTavish settled into a chair. "We agree on that," he said.

"How long have you been here?" Kincaid asked.

MacTavish looked at him with a calm and steady gaze. "Now, that doesn't really interest you, does it?"

Kincaid knew he had made his first false step and alerted himself immediately. "I clearly understand why you don't want to sell," he said. "For very good reasons, I sincerely hope that you don't."

"Why?"

"For one thing, a Chinese-owned hotel could be a prime place to bring in dope."

In a calm, quiet way, MacTavish studied him. "And I'm to believe that you're just a public-spirited citizen. An American by your accent, though it's a bit strange."

In a flash Kincaid saw that MacTavish was much more sophisticated than he had expected. He remembered how much

Portuguese he had spoken during his years in Brazil. It had tinged his voice a little.

"Mr. MacTavish," he said, "I'm about to become the president of an American construction company. We're specialists in designing and building things that fit in with and support the environment."

He waited for a reaction, but MacTavish simply sat still and watched him.

He tried again. "The Hong Kong people have offered to buy you out."

"True."

"But they can't force you to sell."

MacTavish allowed the slightest pause. "If they could, they would. Now, make your proposition."

"Here it is," Kincaid responded, "laid out flat. I'm ready, tonight, to pay you twenty-five thousand dollars, cash on the line, for an option to buy your property if you ever do decide to sell."

"For how long?" MacTavish said.

Kincaid had not intended to include a time limit, but he knew immediately he would have to yield the point. "Five years," he said.

"If I were to sell you the option, who would set the final price?"

"You would—within reason."

When MacTavish's wife came in with the tea, he barely looked at her. "Let me understand," he said. "You're willing to pay me twenty-five thousand for a five-year option only in case I decide on my own to sell."

"That's right."

"Then what do you do, hire a rock band to play outside my window?"

"Absolutely nothing like that. I'll put it in writing."

"And if I choose just to stay here for the next five years?"

"You keep the money."

"I see. You'll have blocked the Chinese from building their hotel."

"Yes. And there'd be no point in pestering you, because if you did decide to sell, I'd be holding the option."

"In that case, you could sell it to them for a very good price."

"That's probably right," Kincaid admitted. "But I wouldn't. I'm willing to put in a clause to that effect."

"Then what are your plans?"

"With respect, that's my business."

MacTavish accepted a cup of strong tea from his wife. "I'll think about it," he said. "Draw up the paper and let me read it."

"Fair enough." Kincaid had a document ready in his pocket, but it did not include the five-year clause. Also, he knew by now what a mistake it would be to appear too slick. He sat still and drank his tea.

"Come and see me tomorrow," MacTavish said when he was ready.

"I will," Kincaid promised. He knew then that his fish was hooked.

At a steady pace the unmarked police car rolled westward across the North Island. It was painted a conservative blue that drew little attention; only a close observer could have spotted the evidence of radio gear inside or anything else to show its official function.

Superintendent Winston drove it with effortless ease. In an emergency situation he could make it do things that few drivers would dare to attempt, but he had no need for that advanced skill as he came close to staying within the speed limit. Beside him Peter Ferguson took in the passing scenery.

It had been quiet inside the car for several miles when Winston broke the silence. "There are some things about New Zealand that most outsiders don't understand," he began. "You might want to know about them."

"By all means," Peter said.

"We are not as stuffy and stiff-necked as some people think. It's just that we have certain priorities, and to us they're important. For more than twenty years we've stopped the construction of high rises, not because they aren't efficient, but they don't go with the kind of country we have. Our schools must provide so much open green or playing area for each student they enroll. As a result, we're insulated from urban blight and overdevelopment."

He stopped, continuing his driving with both hands smoothly on the wheel.

"Peter," he continued, "I was in your country not too long ago and drove south from Miami toward Key West. Florida is a beautiful state, but what I saw was an endless parade of neon signs, billboards, motels, fried chicken stands, parking lots, and liquor stores. To me it looked obscene."

"It probably was," Peter agreed. "Too much commercialism will ruin anything."

"It's certainly destroyed that part of Florida. We don't want the same thing happening here. That's why we aren't interested in overpromoting our tourist industry, or having it done for us."

"I won't argue," Peter said.

Winston turned at an intersection onto a new road. "Now, about Rotorua, where we're going," he continued. "It's one of the prime tourist centers in the whole country. It's an active thermal area with many hot springs and quite a few geysers. We have one geyser that is supposed to have reached twelve hundred feet; it's dormant now. And there's a geyser that goes off every morning at ten-thirty."

"I don't know much about geysers, but that sounds odd to me. How can a geyser run by the clock?"

"I can't say, Peter, but fortunately it isn't a police matter. More important at the moment, we have word that an aggressive buying team from Pricane arrived today in Auckland. After Mr. Kincaid meets with them, we may have to step in and explain some points of New Zealand law."

"Don't expect them to be too impressed," Peter warned.

"We quite understand that. From information received, we expect them to come to Rotorua very soon."

"That figures," Peter said. "What am I to do?"

"Does Kincaid know you by sight?"

"No, I've never met him."

"Good. What I want to do, Peter, is to set you up in Rotorua as an American tourist who has plenty of money, lots of time, and a local girlfriend. I'll take care of supplying the young lady."

"I can carry that off," Peter said. "I've been alone for a while. Your girl will look the part, I assume."

"You can count on it," Winston assured.

Peter remembered how vastly experienced Pricane was in the international field. The acquisitions went steadily on, whether those being taken over liked it or not. The buying team would know a dozen ways around the laws. Also, it would be backed by huge resources of cash, the universal language of power and authority.

When they drove into Rotorua, Peter discovered that it was quite a small place and visibly quiet. It, too, seemed to be two generations behind the United States, but he was beginning to like this different way of life.

"At the police station we'll put you in a cab—it'll look better that way when you arrive at the hotel. The Grand Establishment is a comfortable place; you'll enjoy it. By the way, your lady friend will be in the next room. I trust you'll observe due discretion."

Peter smiled a little grimly. "If I must," he answered. "Frankly, I'm not very familiar with policewomen."

"They're well trained; many of them work undercover. They also appear in uniform and perform various police functions, including patrol."

As he finished speaking, he turned into an ample parking lot behind the police building. "The cab will be here directly," Winston said. "We have an arrangement with the driver. Here he is now."

Peter transferred his gear to the cab and got inside. The driver started up, drove around a few blocks, and then pulled up in front of the modest-appearing Grand Establishment. Peter got out, let the driver set out his bags for him, and handed over some money.

The lobby was comfortable and had a warm atmosphere. He could see an inviting bar down a short hall to his right, and there was an attractive restaurant opposite the reception desk. He picked up a pen and gave the clerk behind the counter his name.

"Yes, sir, we have your reservation," the clerk said, and handed over a key. At that moment Peter did his first piece of detective work: he noted that the clerk had not used his name, as would have been customary. Therefore he had been briefed: presumably people wouldn't be calling him "Mr. Ferguson" all over the hotel.

The clerk spoke again. "The lady you were expecting has already checked in. I believe she's in the bar. Shall I hold your bags here?"

The hint was very clear. Doing his best to appear casual, he walked into the bar and looked about. Then he stopped.

There was only one single woman in the bar, and she was seated very close to where he was standing.

"Hello," Jenny Holbrook said. "Are you looking for me?"

CHAPTER 22

Peter sat down. He looked at the young woman across from him and said, "Winston told me that I'd like the policewoman he picked for me. He was right."

"He didn't tell you whom to expect?"

"He didn't. He's cagey that way."

Jenny pursed her lips in a gentle smile. "He and Dad have been good friends for many years. They went to school together." She changed her tone a little. "Why don't you get yourself a drink? I'll wait."

Peter went to the bar and returned with a highball in his hand. "So you're a cop," he said.

"A reservist, on call when I'm needed."

"So you'll be reporting on me."

In the background there was a steady hum of conversation. A clink of glasses could be heard, and then a short burst of hearty laughter.

"Now you're assuming things," she said when she was ready. "I put in my reports only what's of official interest; I never go beyond that. Understood?"

Peter took a little of his drink. "I've been told that you'll pose as my New Zealand girlfriend, in whom I'm very interested. Have you any ideas?"

Jenny played with the stem of her glass. "We can work that out as we go, I think. Just pretend that you really like me, and I'll do the same toward you." She looked at him with a heart-stopping smile, in case anyone was watching. "But that doesn't mean that we'll be sleeping together."

"I've been cautioned," Peter told her.

Jenny changed the subject. "Peter, a high-powered Pricane executive called Kincaid is booked into this hotel. Our job will be to keep an eye on him."

"Any suggestions?" he asked.

"After breakfast, I think we should go sight-seeing. Anything else wouldn't look right."

"If we do, how will we know what's going on?"

Jenny's hand patted his very lightly. "Don't worry about that. I also work for Mount Cook, remember? Rotorua is one of our destinations, and I have friends here and there." Peter sensed that the conversation was over. It had been a long day, and despite Jenny's company, he was about ready to call it enough. He finished his drink and then asked, "Shall we go?"

As they passed through the lobby, he retrieved his bags and carried them himself. With Jenny beside him he climbed the stairs, located his room, set down his bags and put the key in the lock. Then he turned to her. "How long is this likely to last?" he asked.

"I don't know. A day or two—or it could be longer." She teased him a little. "I hope you don't mind too much."

He was very tempted to reach for her as he had done once before, but he caught the sound of footsteps approaching down the corridor. Almost before he realized it, she had her arms around him, her lips pressed on his.

He responded immediately, holding her close while someone passed them in the corridor. He heard the sound of a door being unlocked, then closed a moment later.

Gently she separated herself from him. "You never know—" she began.

"And you're supposed to be my girlfriend," he finished for her. "By the way, unless I get to do that at least once a day, I become savage and uncontrollable."

"I'll bear that in mind."

When she had gone, he shut the door behind her, shucked off his clothes, washed quickly, and then fell into bed. He remembered he had forgotten to leave a wake-up call, but before he could make up his mind to get up and do it, he was already asleep.

It was only a little after eight in the morning when he went down to the dining room. The hostess took him in charge and led him to a table where Jenny was already installed. Her food had been served, and she had begun eating.

"Good morning," she said. "You looked tired last night so I decided to let you sleep for a while."

"Thanks." He took the seat opposite her and ordered breakfast. When his meal came, he ate almost all of it. As soon as he was finished, Jenny became businesslike. "I know my way around Rotorua, so we won't need a guide. We have a rental car on the lot; I took it out in your name."

For a moment he wondered how she had managed that; then his attention was caught by a tall, well set-up man whose pleasant smile had flattered the hostess he was following. "That's Kincaid," Jenny said. "He came in by car last night."

"Jenny, you don't let much get past you, do you?"

She waited while the waitress refilled their coffee cups. "When I'm on the job, I do the best that I can," she answered. "It's expected of me."

Silently they finished the coffee; then she led the way outside. From two or three different directions plumes of stark white steam reached upward into the clear blue sky. "All of this area is thermal," Jenny said. "There are fumaroles, boiling ponds, vents, hot springs, and geysers. A lot of the heat is tapped and used commercially." She handed him a set of keys.

At her direction he drove south down a narrow but well-maintained road. He enjoyed the drive and had no difficulty assuming his role as an interested tourist. It was more fact than fiction.

Following Jenny's directions, he turned off onto a large parking lot in front of a reception center. As he got out of the car, the smell of sulfur was strong in the air.

As soon as they started down a well-prepared pathway, they encountered many forms of thermal activity. Steam hissed under pressure from encrusted holes in the ground, and boiling water heavily tinged with sulfur flowed from bubbling springs as gas

115

vents poured out a continuous reminder of the inferno that was somewhere deep underground. It was an experience that combined sights, sounds, and a variety of odors that were foreign to all but a few spots on earth.

"Is there any sign of all this cooling off?" Peter asked.

Jenny shook her head. "The build-up around some of the geysers shows that they've been active for hundreds of years."

After a few more minutes she took Peter's hand. "We'd better start back if we want to see the ten-thirty eruption," she said.

A short drive took them to another parking lot, where a few cars and two buses were already on hand. A wooded pathway led to a small cleared area where logs had been placed to serve as benches. They faced an area of rock hardpan, in the center of which a six-foot-high geyser cone was emitting a steady flow of rising steam. Forty or fifty people were seated on the logs. One of them was Kincaid, talking to an older couple beside him. Peter sensed that the man from Pricane was not just being sociable—he would be ferreting out information.

From somewhere deep underground a gurgle could be heard; then the flow of steam began to increase rapidly. Almost to the minute a tentative jet of water rose a few feet and then fell back. Another followed; then through a cloud of steam a solid column of water shot upward, crested, and began to fall back onto the hardpan. A deep-throated roar came with the first burst and continued for the thirty seconds or more that the geyser continued to erupt. Then the column of water fell off dramatically and ceased while the steam continued to rise into the clear sky.

The spectators rose to go. Most of them got into the waiting buses; Kincaid had a rental car that he drove away himself. Peter noted with satisfaction that he started off on the right-hand side of the road and had to correct himself. The man might be a top executive, but he had his flaws.

They took lunch at a restaurant halfway back toward Rotorua. As soon as they had been served, Peter stated what was on his mind. "Kincaid didn't go to see that geyser just for his own entertainment; he was there for a purpose. Who owns it?"

"It belongs to one of the hotels," Jenny answered.

"Then that's his target. A hotel with a tame geyser would fit

116

in perfectly with Pricane's plans, because they don't like to leave anything to chance. Buses could be scheduled in and out with no wasted time or increased costs if there was a delay. The people could be herded around faster and profits increased that way."

Jenny nodded. "Winston will want to know that," she said.

As they drove back to Rotorua, Peter reminded himself that although Jenny had been assigned to be his companion, the biggest mistake he could make would be to take her for granted. "Will you have dinner with me this evening?" he asked.

"That's already in the cards."

"But in the line of duty," Peter said. "I'm asking you to be my guest—my date."

She gave him a smile. "I accept with pleasure." Then she said, "I have to tell you—we're booked for a dinner and a show later. It's with a tourist group."

"I had hoped we could be by ourselves," he began, then he got it. "Kincaid," he finished.

She nodded her appreciation. "I've been given his schedule. We just happen to be in the same party."

When they returned to the hotel, Jenny went to a telephone. Peter took advantage of her absence to stop at the desk. "I'd like to send some flowers to Miss Holbrook," he told the clerk. "Is it too late to arrange it for this evening?"

"We can have something suitable delivered to her in about forty minutes, give or take."

"Please do that."

The clerk picked up a pen. "What would you like on the card?"

" 'To my dinner date.' "

The clerk wrote and went to his phone. Moments later, Jenny reappeared. "Since we're going out tonight, why don't you go up and rest for a while? I'm planning to do the same thing," she said.

Shortly after six he met her in the lobby. She had a sprig of fresh flowers pinned to her dress. She was stunning, a fact that did not escape the desk clerk or the several other people in the lobby. Peter claimed her proudly and asked, "Do we dine here or elsewhere?"

"Elsewhere," she answered. "I made a reservation."

The dinner was a new experience for him: a Maori *hangi*, in which the cooking was done in a natural hot spring. The guests were seated in two long rows facing each other. Kincaid positioned himself in the middle of one of the rows; Peter picked a spot five seats down from him with Jenny opposite him. The sulfurous water gave the food an odd taste, but it was still quite good.

Despite the novelty and the very different nature of the occasion, Peter did not pay a great deal of attention to his meal. As he looked at Jenny opposite him, his mind was fixed on the fact that she was the most captivating girl he had ever known. If she was aware of his admiration, she did not let it show.

When they had finished, they followed the tourist bus, which took the main group to a Maori show obviously intended for a tourist audience. After the show he took Jenny back to the hotel, bought her a drink in the bar, and then saw her up to her room for the night. He was rewarded with a warm kiss; when he put his arms around her to receive it, it was hard for him to let go.

Later, as he lay on his bed trying to go to sleep, he could not get her out of his mind.

C H A P T E R   23

The careful watch that had been kept throughout New Zealand for the two Australians was stepped up in intensity after the attack on Constable Fred Fisher. He was reported in hospital with a brain concussion, burns, and severe glandular injuries, the result of his having been groin-kicked. The brutality of his attackers had created a tidal wave of rage that reached into every part of the well-disciplined police department.

Its sworn members took out their frustration by working long hours overtime. Firearms were issued in recognition of the fact that unarmed constables were not able to deal with the kind of men who had assaulted Fisher, despite their physical courage and devotion to duty.

Peter was halfway through his breakfast when Jenny slid into the booth beside him. "Morning," she said with a briskness that indicated she had not just come from her room.

"Morning," he responded. "Been for a walk?"

"Not far."

He remembered that the police station was only a short distance away. "And who did you talk to?" he asked, knowing the answer already.

"Hubert."

"So it's 'Hubert' now, is it?"

She signaled to a waitress, who nodded in acknowledgment. "He's my godfather," she said. "Now, I've news for you. We're going to the Bay of Islands. You'll love it there—it's gorgeous. We're booked on the late morning flight."

"We're through here, then?"

"For the time being. I passed on what we'd learned and what you told me. One other thing: Kincaid went out last night quite late. The night clerk had to open the door for him."

"Do they lock up here at night?"

"Usually. Kincaid was gone about an hour. He met with someone, another man. We don't know who he is yet."

"But you expect to find out."

"Of course. Meanwhile, we're off to have a good time at the Bay." She paused a moment. "I think I can promise you that you'll like it."

The call came in to the one-man Russell police station before eight in the morning, but Constable Pettibone was already there. During the almost forty years that he had served with the police, he had never been known to be derelict in his duty. In appearance he was a well-formed man and stood more than six fet tall in his always crisp uniform. His hair had been white for some time, and his face betrayed the fact that he would never see sixty again. The unwelcome specter of retirement loomed before him, but he refused to give in to it, even so much as an inch. Regardless of the time, place, or circumstance, Constable Orin Pettibone was fully prepared to carry out his duties with distinction, as was his custom.

119

The few strained words that Mrs. MacTavish spoke to him over the phone engaged his immediate attention. "I shall be there at once," he declared. "Meanwhile, have you called the doctor?"

He listened for a second or two and then issued an order. "Call him directly. It's important that you do so for several reasons. Otherwise, leave everything to me."

The moment the line was free, Pettibone put through a quick call to his superior. "I have a reported death under questionable circumstances," he reported. "I'll look into it at once and advise."

Since the inspector knew Pettibone thoroughly, he saw no need to send reinforcements to a place as quiet as Russell. During his long career Pettibone had never put in for promotion, but he enjoyed the full confidence of some very high-ranking members of the department.

None of this was in the constable's mind as he drove his official car the short distance to the MacTavish home. As he strode up the path to the modest cottage, the door was opened by a woman who seemed about to collapse.

Pettibone was at her side in a moment. "There, now, Mrs. MacTavish," he said as he almost literally held her up. "There's no need for that. I'm here now."

He helped the distraught woman into the small living room and put her into a comfortable chair. "Now, tell me just what you found." His voice was considerate, even gentle, but it also carried a note of command.

Mrs. MacTavish somehow found the words she had to speak. "When I woke this morning, my husband was not in the house. I didn't see him outside, and the car was parked in its usual place. So I looked in the garden."

Pettibone immediately visualized the small garden that reached to the edge of the almost-sheer cliff. Ned MacTavish liked his drop of drink now and then, but the constable had never seen him when he was not in possession of himself. A drunken fall, in his considered judgment, was out of the question.

As soon as Mrs. MacTavish was ready to speak again, he was all attention. "I walked up to the end, and there I saw a break in the hedge. It wasn't there yesterday."

Pettibone felt a chill run through him. "You have called the doctor," he confirmed.

"Yes." As she pronounced it, the word was a dead and empty hull.

"Please wait for me." Judging that it would be safe to leave her for a brief interval, Pettibone stepped outside and gave his close attention to the short path that led into the garden. The earth was packed hard and showed no visible traces. In the garden itself the soil had been recently hoed, and footprints were visible. Pettibone dropped to one knee for a closer look; what he saw gave him added concern.

Walking carefully to one side, he approached the small break in the protective hedge that marked the edge of the garden plot. He counted fourteen broken twigs in the hedge; all of them had been pushed outward. Although there was almost no ground at all between the hedge and the edge of the cliff, Pettibone stepped over, and by holding on to one of the larger hedge plants, he managed to lean far enough out into space to look down.

Ned MacTavish was halfway down the steep face, where his body had been caught by a small stunted tree that had somehow managed to find a roothold in that dangerous place.

Prudence demanded that Pettibone go back for a rope and phone for some help from the hotel, knowing that it would be forthcoming at once. But that would take a few minutes, and even that amount of time could be of the essence. Despite the fact that he was in full uniform and wearing brightly shined street shoes, he turned his face toward the cliff wall and began to work his way down. He knew what he was attempting was highly hazardous, but a man's life could be at stake.

With great care he descended, fighting for fragile footholds with a full awareness that even a slight misstep would send him on a two-hundred-foot plunge down onto the rocks below. But he did not yield to fear, for he had no intention of falling.

When he reached MacTavish, he hooked his left arm around the tough little tree and with his right hand made a swift and expert examination, feeling for a pulse and determining as much as he could about the extent of injuries. He quickly discovered

121

that MacTavish's spine was broken, undoubtedly from the impact against the tree when he fell. There was no question that he was dead—even the feel of his flesh was cool.

There was no possibility that Pettibone could climb either up or down with the body; Tarzan could not have accomplished it. He was planning his next move when he heard a shout from above. He looked up with some care and saw the familiar face of Dr. Willis Humboldt, who had many capabilities in addition to his medical expertise. "Shall I come down?" the doctor shouted.

Rather than announce his findings to the world and possibly to Mrs. MacTavish in particular, Pettibone gestured instead. The doctor understood at once. "I'll fetch a rope," he called down.

Since it was the most prudent thing possible, the constable remained precisely where he was. While he waited, he studied the whole scene and the exact position of the body. It disconcerted him to look down, but he did it because it was his duty.

In a surprisingly short time the doctor was back. A thin nylon rope began to snake its way down the cliff face. When it was low enough, the doctor put a side whip into it that brought it within Pettibone's reach.

It took him only a matter of seconds to tie it expertly under the body's arms with a slip noose in back. When he had finished, he signaled with his free arm. "Mind the footprints!" he called up.

"Right," the doctor responded, and the rope grew tight. Humboldt was not an especially brawny man, but he pulled the body up at a steady pace that did not falter. When the rope came down again, Pettibone tied a bowline-on-a-bight and slipped his arms into the loops. With his safety then virtually guaranteed, he climbed steadily up the almost sheer face without losing his footing even once.

When he reached the top, the doctor grasped his hand to pull him safely over the edge. "Took a bit of a chance, didn't you?" he remarked.

Pettibone had no time for trivialities after what he had read in the soil just inside the hedge. "He's dead," he confirmed.

"Yes."

"It's murder, then," the constable announced. "I'd appreciate it if you'd look after the necessary procedures, and Mrs. MacTavish. I have a lot to do."

While the doctor went to his car to get a covering sheet for the body, Pettibone took out his notebook and began to draw a detailed sketch. When he had completed it, he returned to his own car and came back with a small camera. He took several close-up photographs of the break in the hedge and of the soft ground just in front of it. He focused carefully and adjusted each exposure to insure that the results would be clear and sharp.

By the time he had finished, several other people had appeared on the scene, not to gape but to assist however they could. Two of the men helped load the body into the back of the doctor's station wagon. There were some urgent questions Constable Pettibone wanted to put to Mrs. MacTavish, but he elected to forgo them until even more pressing matters had been dealt with first.

He drove back to the police station, then walked quickly to the hotel next door and spoke with the owner. "Mr. Young," he said without preamble, "I need to talk with you immediately in confidence."

"Understood. Go ahead."

"Ned MacTavish is dead, killed by persons presently unknown. What do you know about any plans to build a new hotel here?"

"Nothing but rumors," Young answered. "A lot of them have been floating around—you must have heard them."

"Earlier I noted a visitor here: American, male, forty-five to fifty. Five-eleven, twelve stone or a bit more, very well dressed."

"Mr. Theodore Kincaid," Young said. "He dined one evening with Superintendent Winston."

"Then we will have a full book on him," Pettibone declared. "Winston is a sound man, very sound indeed. Now, I need help in locating two men, both quite large and heavy, one wearing a size twelve boot, the other thirteen or better. That's all the description I have so far."

"Wait a moment," Young said. "I'm almost sure that Kincaid

123

went up to see Ned one evening. I know for a fact that he showed unusual interest in the bluff area where Ned lived."

Pettibone had his notebook out at once. "Mr. Kincaid's occupation?" he asked.

"President of an American construction company."

"Aha! That would put him in opposition to the others who are reputed to be trying to buy in up here. Do you know his present whereabouts?"

"He left no address."

"Winston will know," Pettibone declared without hesitation. "Thank you. Speak of this conversation with no one."

He returned to the police station, called Whangavel, and reported. "I have a definite homicide with two suspects involved. Both are large men, probably weighing over sixteen stone. The victim is Ned MacTavish, sixty-six, sober, of good reputation, clean record. He leaves a widow who is presently being seen to by neighbors. MacTavish was pushed to his death over a cliff behind his home. His property has been sought by at least two outside interests, reputedly to build a luxury hotel on the site."

He listened to the inspector on the line and responded to a question. "No, thank you, no assistance is needed. I shall conduct the investigation myself with every expectation of success."

Having nothing more to say, he hung up.

CHAPTER 24

In late morning a Norman Islander lined up a short runway that belonged to Mount Cook, dropped its flaps, and landed with smooth efficiency. As soon as the two engines were shut down, the passengers began to deplane. Two elderly ladies went inside the tiny terminal looking for facilities; the rest stood waiting for the small bus that would take them into Waitangi and to the Russell ferry. They had all noted the American and his obviously kiwi girlfriend, but if they had any thoughts concerning their relationship, they kept them to themselves.

Within five minutes the bus rolled in. It dropped off some passengers for the return flight and gathered up its new load. As it made its way through the countryside, the flora everywhere gave evidence of a warmer and more gentle climate. At the end of its run the bus came down a moderate grade and pulled up at the ferry pier.

With Jenny's help Peter collected their baggage and bought tickets for the trip across the bay to Russell. As they walked down the short pier together, the mildness of the day and the smooth water stretching out to embrace so many separate islands intensified his mood of pleasure. He looked at Jenny and wished that she were his. He knew that he was getting ahead of himself and remarked simply, "It's beautiful."

"Yes," she agreed. "I've never been outside New Zealand, but it must be one of the loveliest places anywhere."

Peter turned to her. "I'm very grateful to be here," he said. "I can't believe my own good fortune." If she wanted to read anything into that, she was welcome to do so.

"You're really romantic, aren't you?" she asked.

"I'd feel sorry for anyone who wasn't," he answered.

He was still absorbed by the magnificent panorama when the ferry bumped gently against its dock on the Russell side and it was time for him to come back to earth. He picked up their luggage and carried it easily; fresh new energy seemed to have infused his body, and Jenny walking beside him added to his newfound sense of well-being. In less than five minutes they reached the Duke of Marlborough Hotel.

At the reception desk he put down the suitcase and looked at the attractive woman who was behind it. "Good morning," he said. "I'm Peter Ferguson."

"Yes, Mr. Ferguson, you're expected." She looked at the two of them a scant moment and then consulted her file. "Was that two rooms?" she asked, looking as though perhaps an error had been made.

Before Peter could answer, Jenny spoke. "Do you have one of those nice front ones that overlooks the water?"

"Yes. I have a very nice double, if that will do."

Peter signed the register with his own name and then put the pen down. Jenny picked it up and put her name below his.

The lady handed over a key. "It's just to the left at the top of the stairs. We don't have a porter, I'm afraid."

As Jenny took the key, Peter picked up their bags. "Thank you," he said, and followed her up the stairs.

They had a fine large room, nicely furnished in the style of at least a generation back and the better for it. It was the kind of room that Pricane architects would never have allowed to exist. As Peter looked at it and at Jenny, whose back was turned, he spoke silently to himself: "God preserve New Zealand."

He waited while Jenny adjusted her hair in front of a mirror. When she had finished, she turned and rewarded him with a smile. It was a gentle one, but it quickened his pulse. "Would you like to see the town?"

"Fine," he agreed.

As they came down to the lobby, the receptionist met them at the foot of the stairs. "Have a nice stay," she said. "If there's anything you need, please let me know. I'm the manager; my name is Loraine."

"Everything is just fine," Jenny replied. She walked with Peter toward the doorway, where a tall figure appeared before them. Constable Pettibone looked all of his sixty-plus years, but there was nothing to suggest his age in his bearing as he strode in.

"Good morning," he said. "Miss Holbrook and Mr. Ferguson, I believe."

"That's right," Peter responded, wondering if their sleeping arrangement was about to come under official disapproval. "How did you recognize us?"

Pettibone was fully equal to that. "I have been advised that Miss Holbrook is exceptionally attractive. I wish to speak with both of you for a moment or two."

"Of course," Jenny agreed.

Pettibone led the way to one side, where they were clear of the doorway. "There was a murder here last night," he said. "I am now conducting an investigation."

"How can we help you?" Peter asked.

"Miss Holbrook, I believe you are a reserve police officer."

"Yes."

"And Mr. Ferguson, I have it that you are assisting her."

126

"That's right."

"I'm not wholly clear on why you're here."

Peter looked at Jenny, who nodded. "There's a large American company that's after a desirable hotel site here in Russell," he said. "Because I know this company and how it operates, we were sent here to keep our eyes and ears open. I'm supposed to be a well-off tourist; Miss Holbrook is posing as my girlfriend."

"Is Mr. Kincaid involved in this?"

"Definitely."

"I thought so. Now, I will confide in you. For very good reasons I have forestalled a homicide team coming here. I know the locale and the people, which is a great advantage. But I can use some help, if you're so inclined."

"Please tell us what we can do," Jenny said.

Pettibone glanced about him before he continued. "Last night a long-standing local resident of good reputation was pushed over a cliff behind his home and fell to his death. Perhaps it was intended to appear as an accident, but the deception was obvious."

Peter had a quick thought. "Where exactly did this man live?" he asked.

Pettibone gave him an approving look. "Directly atop the place that's wanted for the hotel site. He owned a piece of property essential to the whole project and didn't wish to sell." He took a fast glance at his watch. "I'm sorry, I have very little time. Miss Holbrook—"

"Jenny, please."

"Good. Orin here. It would be most helpful if you would see to the widow, Mrs. Anne MacTavish, and deal with any possible developments. The house is on the telephone, so you can call the police station at any time."

Jenny understood fully. "I'll be glad to," she said.

"I'll take you up there directly. Ferguson, you can be of great help if you will cover the station for me. I have two men trained to do it, but unfortunately both of them are away. I must have someone to answer the telephone and take messages but not to undertake anything beyond that."

"Where's the station?" Peter asked.

"Directly next door. I'll show you what to do, then I'll take Jenny up to Anne MacTavish."

In the station, which appeared to be a private residence, Pettibone explained the simple telephone circuits and how to reach the constable at Waitangi, at the other end of the ferry, in case of emergency. He laid out writing materials, cautioned Peter not to touch any of the other equipment, and left.

Constable Pettibone then escorted Jenny into the small cottage where Anne MacTavish sat, her eyes red with weeping, in the company of two of her neighbors. "I have brought WPC Holbrook to assist you," he said to the bereaved woman. "She will handle the phone and any callers and do whatever else may be required. If anyone should be so inconsiderate as to call you for any reason other than condolences, she will deal with it."

One of the neighbor ladies rose to go. "Then Anne won't be needing us any longer," she said, and nodded significantly to her companion. Pettibone saw them out the door and then spoke to Anne MacTavish once more. "You can rely on Woman Police Constable Holbrook," he said. "I have a man stationed at the police telephone, and I will be checking with him regularly."

Despite her shock and sorrow, Anne MacTavish was in possession of herself. "Sit down, my dear," she said to Jenny. "I have some tea ready."

"Let me get it," Jenny offered.

That was enough to satisfy Pettibone. He excused himself and left at once, for he had a great deal to do within a short time.

CHAPTER 25

When Superintendent Winston got off his plane from Australia, he was in an encouraged frame of mind. He had talked at length with two men in custody; in the hope of lighter sentences they had given him a good deal of information. Some of it was obvious fiction, but all of it would be thoroughly checked out.

When he stopped in at the airport police office, he was given the very upsetting news of the murder at Russell. His amiable manner vanished as he put in a call to check with the constable in charge. Very few things surprised the superintendent, but he was startled when the phone in Russell was briskly answered in an American voice he recognized at once. "Is this Peter Ferguson?" he asked.

"Yes, it is."

"Winston here. What's going on."

"A man was killed here some time last night, thrown over a cliff behind his home. The local constable is out investigating. Jenny and I had just checked in when he asked for our help. Jenny's up with the victim's wife, and I'm covering the phone here. That's it so far."

"Do you know when the homicide team is due?"

"It isn't. Constable Pettibone is doing everything himself."

"Constable Pettibone. Of course, I understand. What will you do if an emergency call comes in?"

"Call the constable at Waitangi. By the way, thanks for assigning Jenny."

"It's come to that, has it? Well, have a good time." Winston hung up.

Five minutes later, when Pettibone called in, Peter reported his conversation with Winston.

"Thank you, Peter. I shall be in before long," Pettibone said in crisp tones, and hung up.

Almost immediately there was another call. As soon as Peter answered, the woman on the line became suspicious. "This isn't Constable Pettibone."

"No, ma'am, I'm assisting him. My name is Ferguson."

"Constable Ferguson, quite by accident I saw something last night. It isn't much, but I think Constable Pettibone should know."

"By all means; thank you for calling. What shall I tell him?"

Bit by bit he extracted the woman's story. She was a widow who lived at the south end of tiny Russell. She had gone to bed early but being unable to sleep had gotten up to make herself a cup of tea. While drinking it, she had seen a yellow car, possibly a Ford, hit a rill in front of her house. All the local people knew it was there, but the yellow car had hit it hard enough to bounce on its springs. Normally she would have forgotten it, but after hearing about the death of poor Ned MacTavish . . .

Peter thanked her and promised to relay the information as soon as possible. When the phone rang again, the voice on the line was male and American. "Excuse me," the caller began, "but I've just heard some disturbing news. I'm told that a gentleman I know, Mr. Ned MacTavish, has met with a serious accident."

Peter was careful. "Are you a member of the family, sir?"

"No. My name is Kincaid. Mr. MacTavish and I were engaged in a business transaction. Is it true that he's dead?"

Clearly Kincaid already knew. "Yes, it is. We understand that he fell from a cliff in the back of his garden."

"How is Mrs. MacTavish?"

"As well as could be expected." That was safe enough.

Peter was noting down the call when Pettibone strode into the station. He listened to Peter's report, then picked up the telephone and put in a call to the inspector at Whangarel.

"Pettibone here," he said. "I have some preliminary information on the homicide last night. Fairly late in the evening the victim, MacTavish, went for a walk in his garden. He had been offered a business proposition and wanted to ponder it in the open air. Being very tired, his wife went immediately to sleep. She didn't miss him until morning.

"While he was in his garden, MacTavish was attacked by two large and powerful men, who threw him over a cliff at the back of his property. In the doctor's opinion death was instantaneous. I've established that the villains were not local men. They came and went by car. I have reason to believe that they had never before been in Russell."

Pettibone paused to listen.

"Yes, sir," he continued. "I was just coming to that. They were in all probability driving a yellow Ford Cortina, obviously a rental car. I expect to learn the plate number shortly."

As he listened once again, Pettibone showed the faintest signs of annoyance.

"That's very kind of you, sir, but I've only begun my investigation. Now, if you don't mind, I have several things to do." He hung up and turned to Peter. "I fear that I've quite spoiled your holiday," he said, and left.

It was late afternoon when Pettibone came back. He was about to make another telephone report to his superior when Superintendent Winston walked into the room.

Winston stood rubbing his hands together, suggesting to Peter that he belonged in a Dickens novel. "Good afternoon, gentlemen," he said. "I hear we have some trouble."

Constable Pettibone revealed his vast experience by saying nothing, an example Peter was glad to follow. After a second or two had passed, the superintendent turned to Pettibone and put a direct question. "Orin, aren't things getting a bit thick for you?"

The constable's eyes flashed a look that stopped just short of indignation. "Definitely not!" he retorted. "If I require assistance, I will ask for it."

Winston smiled, almost to himself, as if he had tested the waters and found them as expected. "Then perhaps you'll fill me in on how things stand."

"There are two major considerations here with which we have to deal," Pettibone began. "The murder of Ned MacTavish has demanded my first attention. He was a greatly respected man here, and before his death I would have said that he had no enemies. I regret that we no longer have a hangman to deal with his killers after I catch up with them."

"You're not alone," Winston said. "Go on."

"The second matter is the motive for the crime. I know better than to accept a very visible one without also looking for others, but at the moment I'm convinced that Ned was done in because he owned a key piece of land that some very powerful interests want to acquire."

"Why didn't they buy it from him?" Winston asked. "Presumably they would have been able to afford a very substantial figure."

"Ned MacTavish was his own man. That was his home, and he didn't wish to sell. He was very comfortably fixed—I checked with his bank earlier today. He had all he needed, and he wasn't a greedy person."

"The bank was cooperative, I take it."

"Very cooperative, sir. The manager knew perfectly well that I could get the necessary legal authorization. Since time is very critical right now, I put it on the basis of a personal favor as well as a service to poor Ned. In that light I was given the information I needed. Ned and Anne lived very simply, but they had close to a million tucked away."

Pettibone moved to where he was within reach of the telephone. "I asked WPC Holbrook to stay with Anne MacTavish; she is there now."

"Good move," Winston said.

"I then investigated the scene of the crime and took photographs, which will be available shortly. I also made a cast of the footprints for possible use in court. Then I set about a search for witnesses. We have one of two citizens who make a career of observing all they can of what's going on; I started with them."

"Were they helpful?"

"In a negative sense, yes. They had seen nothing, which virtually guarantees that the men I wish to interview didn't pass their houses. Then most fortunately, a young man I know quite well came forward. We had a bit of a chat. He and a young lady were out together last night. They had parked their car where it was well out of sight and were on foot—at first, that is—near the MacTavish home. There is a secluded spot there that is suitable for . . ."

"Romantic involvements?" Winston suggested.

"Well said. My witness spotted the lights of a car coming up the hill. Since he and the girl were well concealed from the roadway, he was not unduly concerned that they would be seen."

"You showed him a photograph?"

"Mixed with some others, yes."

"Excellent," Winston said. "Excellent! I trust you will not be causing this valuable witness any embarrassment."

"Certainly not, sir. Consenting adults they were, which ends the matter as far as I am concerned."

"And me also. Can you make a case against Edward Riley?"

Pettibone addressed himself to Peter. "I should explain that there are two major parts to an investigation such as this. The

132

first is to determine who committed the crime. The second is to assemble enough clear and convincing evidence to win a conviction in Court. Quite often we can identify the villain, but we can't bring him to justice for lack of enough legal evidence or adequate witnesses."

"I understand," Peter said. He already knew that, but thought it best not to say so.

Pettibone turned to the superintendent. "So far I have no case in the legal sense. My witness did not see the actual crime or know of it until this morning."

Winstood stood up. "I know you'll keep on with your very good work. Peter, I'll walk you back to the hotel if you'd like."

"Thank you," Peter said. He took his leave when they arrived at the comfortable old hotel.

He went up to their room and stretched out on the bed, hands behind his head, and allowed himself to relax. He had done too little of that lately. He had almost fallen asleep when the door opened and Jenny came in. He got to his feet and asked, "How did it go?"

Jenny put down her purse and dropped into a chair. "Poor Anne—it's a terrible blow to her. She still can't believe that her husband won't come home and that they will never be together again. The phone rang a lot. Four of the callers asked about buying the property. One of them rang through from Hong Kong."

"How did they find out so soon?" Peter asked. "Unless they were responsible—"

Jenny cut him off. "I thought of that and called Orin. He checked. The Hong Kong people have a local real estate man. When he heard about Ned's death, he phoned them for instructions."

Peter dropped his shoulders. "How did Mrs. MacTavish take it all?"

"She's a brave woman, but it was still terrible for her."

"Of course. Do you want to change for dinner?"

"Yes," Jenny answered. "Why don't you wait for me downstairs?"

He took himself to the bar, where he sat down with a highball.

He had half expected to find Winston there, but the superintendent was nowhere in sight.

When Jenny appeared, Peter saw that she had put on a soft flowered dress and done some subtle things with her makeup. While they had drinks and dinner together, he sorted out his feelings about her. She had intelligence and natural grace of movement, and she was a genuine beauty. He was captivated by her. He couldn't help wondering what life would be like if he could spend a good portion of it in her company. He wasn't at all sure she was available for that—a girl like her had to have scores of friends, including some very special ones. And to her he was, after all, a foreigner.

After dinner they spent some time with a friendly crowd in the bar. Sometime after ten he glanced at Jenny, knowing she had had a trying day. When she gave him a confirming nod, he excused them both, and together they went upstairs. He unlocked the door of their room and then stepped aside to let her enter. It was a very small thing, but she smiled her thanks and waited while he turned on the lights. "Why don't you use the bathroom first?" she suggested.

In response, he took off his coat and tie and hung them up. Then he went in, washed, and prepared himself for bed. "It's all yours," he said as he came out.

As soon as Jenny disappeared, he set out his toilet articles and unpacked the rest of his gear. When he finished, he stepped out of his clothes, snapped off the lights, and climbed into the comfortable bed.

Time dragged a little then until Jenny came out of the bathroom. She had folded her clothes into a neat little packet, which she put carefully on the end of the dressing table; then she turned and walked toward him. Her naked body, made visible by the moonlight, was flawless.

He held up the covers for her as she slid into bed beside him. She had come to him just as she was, without coyness or pretense, and he loved her for it.

She kissed him gently. "Peter, I want you to know something. I just don't—" He silenced her by laying a finger across her lips. "Please don't talk about it."

He put his arm across her shoulder and felt the creamy smoothness of her back. With his thumb and forefinger he massaged the base of her neck, making tiny circles with gentle pressure. "I like that," she said. "Do you do that for all your women?"

He didn't answer. The lay still together, both aware that they had the long hours of the night to spend with each other. The outside world had withdrawn and left them alone.

Presently he drew Jenny even closer to him until their two bodies seemed to form a single whole. He ran his hand down the inviting curves of her buttocks, feeling the radiant warmth of their intimacy. When he knew she was ready for him he raised himself on his elbow and slid her under him as the fire within him continued to grow.

Then he made love to her with all the intensity of his being. He felt no mad rush of passion, only a deep and profound desire to be with her alone and to share equally the growing fulfillment of their union.

CHAPTER 26

As Theodore Kincaid sat over his breakfast in Aukland, he was reviewing in his mind exactly what his next steps should be. His buying team was on the spot, ready to go to work, but certain matters had to be cleared up first.

Leaving these matters open in his mind, he returned to his room to get some work done. It took him until almost two in the afternoon. When he finished, he checked out and took a taxi to the airport, where he waited out his short flight to the Bay of Islands.

It was well into the afternoon when he arrived back at Russell, so he phoned immediately to the MacTavish home. When he had his party, his voice became rich, comforting, and sympathetic. "Mrs. MacTavish, this is Theodore Kincaid. You may recall that I came to see your husband a few days ago."

"Aye. I remember."

"I don't want to disturb you at such a time," he continued, "but despite our short acquaintance, I would like to see your interests protected. For that reason, I would appreciate it if you would allow me to call on you briefly this evening. It is really quite important."

"If you wish," Anne MacTavish answered.

"Thank you very much; I'll try to be worthy of your confidence. Would around eight be satisfactory?"

It was five minutes to eight when he knocked, very carefully, on the door of the MacTavish cottage.

The young woman who opened the door was a considerable surprise. She was far more than attractive: she was beautiful. He surveyed her in two seconds and made a firm resolve to get her into bed no matter what it took to bring her around. He had slept with many beautiful women, but this New Zealand girl was extraordinary."

"Mr. Kincaid?" she said. "Please come in. Mrs. MacTavish is waiting for you."

As she walked ahead of him for only a few steps, he analyzed her figure and gave her top marks. He had been looking forward to sleeping with Susie again, but this new girl completely changed the outlook of the game.

Anne MacTavish, who was just as he had remembered her and wearing the same clothes, got up to greet him. "Thank you, Jenny," she said. "Please sit ye down, Mr. Kincaid. Will you have some tea?"

When the amenities were completed, Kincaid began. "Mrs. MacTavish, as I told your husband, God rest him, I am about to become the president of an American construction company of a quite unusual kind. We are very much concerned with the environment. For more than thirty years everything we have designed and built has been planned to add to, not detract from, the place where it was put up. This is a very strong policy that we have never violated."

"That's very creditable," his hostess said.

"Mrs. MacTavish, when it came to my attention that certain foreign interests—I believe they are Chinese—want to build a large tourist hotel on more or less this very spot, I realized at once that it very easily could be a monstrosity that would virtually destroy the unspoiled beauty of this wonderful region."

"My husband was very concerned about that."

"I certainly admire and respect him for that," Kincaid continued, "and I'm sure he realized that this piece of property is important to the hotel builders. They could go around it if necessary, but that would leave you in a terrible position—literally surrounded by a high rise that would cut off everything but your own lot."

"They can nay do that," Anne MacTavish said. "Our property goes all the way down to the water and a wee bit offshore. The cliff face is no use. It killed my husband, but no one can touch it while it's ours."

Kincaid noted that she spoke of her husband as though he were still living. He would prick that balloon if and when it became necessary.

"Now I would like to say why I am here," he went on. He leaned forward and became a sympathetic friend. "I told your husband that I would pay him twenty-five thousand dollars for an option to buy your property if you ever decide to sell."

"For a period of five years," Anne MacTavish added.

She was being just a little sharper than Kincaid had expected, but he was not worried. If he couldn't take an elderly woman who had been living for years in semi-isolation, he was not the man he knew himself to be.

"Mrs. MacTavish, your husband and I reached an agreement in principle. Now that this terrible thing has happened, I want to assure you that I will keep my word. The twenty-five thousand is yours whenever you are ready to receive it."

Quietly, keeping in the background, Jenny refilled the teacups. She forced the break in Kincaid's selling speech to make sure that the elderly woman in her care was not being pressured. Anne MacTavish, however, seemed to be in full command of herself in all respects. "And why is it that you are making this offer, Mr. Kincaid?"

Kincaid had been expecting that question and was fully prepared to answer it. "I'm going to be very honest with you, Mrs. MacTavish, because that's the only way I will do business. This is a magnificent part of New Zealand. Someday there will be a hotel here—it's inevitable. When that time comes, we would like to be the design consultants. I don't want to see the Hong Kong speculators come in and push up a high-rise monstrosity that will ruin the beauty of the Bay of Islands forever."

"Five years is not a long time," Anne said. "You could lose your money."

Kincaid nodded his head. "I know that, but the important thing is to be sure that the Hong Kong people are stopped. They will probably apply every possible kind of pressure, but as soon as they learn that this property is under option, they will have no choice but to withdraw."

There was a knock on the door; Jenny went to answer. She came back into the room with Peter behind her. "Anne," she said. "I'd like you to meet a very close friend of mine, Peter Ferguson."

At her mention of the name, Kincaid reacted in spite of himself. He got to his feet automatically as Jenny, with seeming innocence, concluded, "Mr. Kincaid—Mr. Ferguson."

"I've heard your name," Kincaid said as, out of necessity, he shook hands.

"And I know yours," Peter replied. "This is quite a change from South America, isn't it?"

As Kincaid sat down he made a determined effort to recover his poise. Ferguson definitely knew who he was and why he was in New Zealand. There was something that the icy-minded Lloyd in the Pricane tower had not foreseen. But that didn't matter: if he failed now, Kincaid's own head would roll.

Jenny was not through. "Anne, Mr. Ferguson is a special consultant to the minister of tourism."

The title was new to Peter, but in his early youth he had learned, if a ball came his way, to catch it and hang on. "I came by," he said, "because we're most interested in any transactions you may have with Mr. Kincaid."

Anne nodded. "Then perhaps, Mr. Ferguson, you'll be able to advise me."

Kincaid could have strangled Peter with his bare hands. He made a quick decision to appear amiable for the moment and wait for his opportunity.

"Peter, would you like some tea?" Jenny asked.

"Yes, thank you."

Kincaid opened his counterattack. "What brings you to New Zealand, Mr. Ferguson?"

"Business and recreation," Peter answered.

138

Kincaid did not challenge that. "I hear you've inherited a piece of land," he said, still in his agreeable manner.

"A station, actually," Peter replied.

"How large is it?"

"Something around forty thousand acres."

Kincaid maneuvered a fresh opening. "Mr. Ferguson, I presume you know that some very aggressive Hong Kong interests want to put up a large hotel in this area."

"Yes. I understand they're after this very spot." The moment he stopped, he knew that he had walked into that one—he had given Kincaid the exact response he had wanted.

While Jenny brought in fresh tea, Kincaid made his next move. "As you may not know, I recently resigned my former position to accept the presidency of an ecologically minded construction firm with a fifty-year reputation for respecting the environment."

"I've heard of it," Peter said.

"You know also that Mr. and Mrs. MacTavish were approached several times to sell their property."

"We dinna care to do that," Anne said.

Kincaid acknowledged her at once. "I well understand. This was your home, and you were happy here." Maintaining his facade of cordiality, he turned to Peter. "What I am offering, Mr. Ferguson, is twenty-five thousand dollars for a five-year option on this property, should Mrs. MacTavish ever decide to sell."

"Should I take it, Mr. Ferguson?" Anne asked.

"You should have good legal advice first," Peter answered. "I know a man you can trust."

The atmosphere of polite conversation vanished abruptly. Kincaid's outer manner did not change, but when he spoke his voice was abruptly sharp and hard. "Mrs. MacTavish, I know a great deal about this man. He is not here for the reasons he gave you—he lied. He came here originally to attempt to defraud some important New Zealand investors." Kincaid burned Peter with a look that was intended to bore through him. "What is more, Mrs. MacTavish, I happen to know that he was detained by the police recently on very serious charges."

Peter sat quietly and kept his composure. Kincaid's skilled use

139

of half-truths made a complete denial impossible. The Smiling Assassin had lived up to his reputation.

He looked at Anne MacTavish and for the first time saw shrewdness in her eyes. "Ye did say that ye came here for recreation, Mr. Ferguson," she said.

Peter was very careful. "Right now I'm seeing New Zealand in the company of Miss Holbrook."

Anne MacTavish nodded. "Aye, that would be recreation," she agreed. "Now, what can you tell me about this Mr. Kincaid? I heard you speak about South America."

Jenny looked at him also waiting to hear his answer.

"For several years Mr. Kincaid has been in Brazil, managing a division of the same conglomerate that would like to acquire this land.

"One like Trans-America, or Gulf and Western?"

That jolted him; he had not expected her to know that much about American business. "The Pricane Industries," he answered.

"Are these the people who want our property?"

"Yes. That's why Mr. Kincaid is here, and why he wants to pay you money."

Kincaid appeared to relax: he put the palms of his hands together and smiled. "Mrs. MacTavish, I resigned from Pricane to accept the presidency of Swarthmore and Stone—I told you that. I've wanted a new connection for some time. Now, I've made a completely open and generous offer just for an option on your property *if* you ever decide to sell. Can I be any fairer than that?" He opened his briefcase, carefully took out a check, and laid it on the coffee table.

Anne shifted in her chair and looked toward Jenny. "You would know," she said. "Did the police arrest Mr. Ferguson?"

"No, Anne. They think highly of him."

"How would you know?" Kincaid asked.

"I'm a policewoman," Jenny replied.

Peter smiled—Kincaid had certainly walked into that one. It was a good time for him to make his own move. "Mrs. Mac-Tavish, your police here are unarmed, and they don't have much of the sophisticated equipment we do, such as helicopters.

140

I suspect that they're underbudgeted, but the ones I have met are intelligent and dedicated people."

"Constable Pettibone," Anne said.

"Constable Pettibone for sure. The police know all about Pricane, and they also know something about Swarthmore and Stone." He glanced at Kincaid, who for the first time appeared off balance.

"Tell me," Anne said.

"Swarthmore and Stone has a good reputation and has had it for fifty years. Recently, against its strong opposition, another company is trying to take it over."

"Can they make them sell out like that?"

"Yes," Peter answered. "Sometimes they can. Especially a large conglomerate that has huge cash resources available."

Anne MacTavish looked at Kincaid. "It's Pricane, isn't it?" she said. "And you still work for them." She picked up his check, looked at it, and then handed it back. "This property isn't for sale—or for option."

Kincaid got to his feet and picked up his briefcase. "Thank you for your time," he said. He was holding himself in tight check as he turned toward the door.

Peter got up also. "I'll see him off."

When they were both outside, Kincaid turned face to face with Peter. His voice was controlled, but there was burning, suppressed anger in it. "Exactly what's your game?" he asked.

"Right now," Peter answered, "I'm with the New Zealand Department of Tourism." Then he changed the topic abruptly. "You know damned well that with her husband dead—murdered on the property—that poor woman may not want to live here anymore."

"Then I'll make her a very good offer," Kincaid snapped back. "Now, try to get this through your skull: Whenever a deal like this comes up, large or small, Pricane always wins. *Always.* We have the resources and the know-how to make things happen our way. You can't stop us, and neither can anyone else, so quit making an ass of yourself trying."

Peter knew that Kincaid was deliberately needling him.

"You'll go to any lengths, then, to put this deal through?"

Kincaid looked at him with contempt. "We control a lot of politicians through our campaign contributions and lobbies, but we don't hire hit men. So don't try to blame MacTavish's death on us."

"That's up to the police," Peter said.

Kincaid's voice hardened to a cutting edge. "We're going to be successful here—I'm seeing to it. The New Zealand tourist business is going to be a Pricane division. And it will be a damned profitable one, the way I'm going to run it."

CHAPTER 27

With heightened intensity the New Zealand police kept up a continuous watch for the Australians wanted for the murder of Ned MacTavish and the attack on Constable Fred Fisher. All sailings of the ferries between the North and South Islands were covered. All crew members who had contact with the passengers were alerted; photographs of the wanted men were posted out of view of the public. All car rental agencies were covered, and all passenger flights, foreign or domestic, were thoroughly checked.

Meanwhile, a systematic search of the whole country was undertaken. In all of the smaller communities the local constables kept a sharp eye out for any men at all whom they did not know and whose business was not clearly evident. A special task force combed through Auckland; by the end of a week there was good reason to believe that the suspects were not in that city.

Hamilton, Christchurch, Wellington, and other population centers were given the same attention. Even as far south as Invercargill the search went on, but without result.

Shortly after five on a Monday afternoon, when traffic was reaching a peak, two men drove into a filling station south of Christchurch. They said very little and paid quickly in cash after their tank had been filled. They did nothing whatever to attract attention to themselves, but the operator of the station had a son who was a police constable in Wellington. Since filling stations are relatively few and far between in New Zealand, they had all been covered and sets of photographs had been distributed.

As soon as the two men had driven away, the station owner looked once more at the pictures he had hidden under his cash drawer and then immediately phoned the police. "Two hearties just left my station, going south on one," he reported. "I took them for Aussies, and they could be the blokes in the pictures you left me."

That triggered an immediate, full-scale response. A fast call was put through to the police station at Ashburton, the first community of any size on the way south. A description of the car was given, but to his chagrin the station owner had failed to note the plate number.

The response from Ashburton had been well planned. A traffic warden's unit was dispatched northbound to spot the wanted car and radio back the moment it was located. In view of the known violent tendencies of the wanted men, arms were issued to those qualified to carry them, and available radio-equipped cars were dispatched with two officers in each one.

The traffic warden made all possible speed northward, hoping to cross the long bridge at Rakaia before the wanted car got there. If the suspects were to cross the water first, there was a small maze of roads branching off that they could then use. As he approached the bridge, he slowed down to normal patrol speed; three miles beyond it, he saw a car that fitted the description of the wanted vehicle. When it was safely behind him, he radioed the information and supplied the license number.

Within two minutes a police ambush was set up and ready. When the suspect car reached it, a roadblock forced it to stop. As it did so, two patrol units swung in behind, and armed constables appeared on both sides of the road. The two occupants were ordered to put their hands on the windshield in front of them. Swiftly and efficiently, they were taken out of their car as the back-up force from Christchurch rolled onto the scene. The car was searched; when a handgun was recovered from the glove compartment, the suspects were taken into custody.

Shortly after they had been put into cells in Christchurch,

their identities were confirmed. The police had good reason to congratulate themselves—it was the first major break in a massive case.

At ten-fifteen that evening one of the suspects was taken from his cell and shown into a room where a stockily built man was waiting. "My name is Winston," he said. "Sit down and make yourself comfortable, because we're going to have quite a long talk."

When Peter awoke he lay still, content to luxuriate in the warm wonderful presence of Jenny Holbrook beside him. When she awoke, he smiled at her, then deliberately waited for her to speak first.

"Good morning, Peter," she said quite simply.

"Good morning, Jenny."

She lay quietly for a few moments. Then she spoke again, with a quiet sincerity in her voice. "Peter, I told you last night—"

He raised a hand to stop her.

"I know, Jenny. They say that a woman always knows, but a man knows some things, too. And I know what a precious, rare privilege it is for me to be here with you."

She smiled then, resting her head on her left arm, the rest of her body covered by the bedding.

"I want to say it anyway," she told him. "I wasn't a virgin, you know that, but you're only the third man in my life. When I was seventeen, I had a terrible crush on a boy I knew, and—well." She stopped, and he knew enough not to interrupt her thoughts. "For weeks after that I was terribly afraid that I might be pregnant. I was terrified every day until I was sure."

"I can understand that," Peter said. "Especially in a place as small as Queenstown."

"You do understand, then," Jenny continued. "After that I never took any more chances; I was a very good girl. Then, a long time after that, there was a boy I had grown up with, someone I liked very much. Nothing was said, but it was pretty well understood that we were going to be married."

"I can't imagine how he let you get away." He meant that very sincerely.

144

"There was an accident," Jenny said. "For a while they didn't know if he would ever walk again or not. He felt that he wasn't a man anymore. I couldn't stand seeing him suffer like that."

"So you gave him the gift he needed, to reassure him."

"It's very nice of you to put it like that. Anyhow, I know that times have changed now, even here in New Zealand. And—" she paused significantly—"I like you very much."

"The man who was hurt, the one you helped so much. Would that be Ray O'Malley's son?"

She looked at him steadily, gathering her own thoughts together. "Yes," she said. "He's a wonderful guy, but he's got a stubborn pride. He told me flat out that he wouldn't ask me to marry a cripple."

"How is he now?"

"Very much better; he gets along quite well with just a cane. Now, Peter, we have to be up and about."

"Immediately?" he asked.

"Well, pretty soon."

When they came down to breakfast almost an hour later, Constable Pettibone was waiting patiently for them in the lobby. Together the three of them went into the dining room. After they were seated, Pettibone declared, "This occasion will be my pleasure, even though I can't put it on my expense account."

"I can," Peter said.

"But you're not going to," Pettibone retorted. "Jenny's company is more than enough reward."

She gave him a particularly radiant smile and then said, "Since you were waiting for us, you must have some news."

Pettibone responded with a crisp nod. "To start, I have completed my immediate investigation of Ned MacTavish's tragic death. The persons responsible have been identified, and the evidence necessary to convict them is being rapidly assembled. Some good witnesses have been located."

"Congratulations," Peter said.

"Thank you. Now, something of perhaps greater interest to both of you. Late yesterday afternoon two members of the Australian gang of villains were captured on the South Island. This is a major break. Hubert Winston has been questioning them."

"When he gets through, you should be way ahead," Peter said.

"I fully agree—Winston is a remarkably able man. I spoke with him by phone early this morning. He had been up all night. He advised me that the persons in custody are not those who did in poor Ned, and they weren't responsible for the attack on Fred Fisher. However, they are being held on a murder charge—they took part in the killing of Will Mahoney."

For a few seconds Peter could not place the name, although he knew he had heard it at one time. Pettibone read him out. "Mahoney was the man thrown onto the bonnet of your car."

An electric sensation ran the length of Peter's spine; now a lot of questions were going to be answered.

Pettibone continued. "Mr. Winston asked me to pass the suggestion that you return to Queenstown."

"How much time have we got?" Jenny inquired.

"Enough to have your meal, pack, and catch the ferry for the airport bus." Pettibone paused and let his official manner slip for a moment. "This is a very beautiful place," he said. "It's a place where almost anyone could be happy. It's also the reason why I have never put in for a promotion that would take me away. I wouldn't blame you if you didn't want to leave."

"I don't," Peter admitted, "but since things seem to be coming to a head, I'll go where they want me to be."

Pettibone rose to his feet. "You'll be back," he assured, "and I'll be pleased to see you. We must come to know one another better." As Peter stood up he shook hands with old-fashioned courtesy before he turned and strode out of the room.

As they flew south toward Christchurch, Peter knew that his idyll of sharing a bed with Jenny was for the moment over. They had had a rare intimacy in the romantic setting of the Bay of Islands, but he could not expect it to continue so much closer to her home.

In Christchurch they stayed in separate rooms at the Claridge Hotel. During the long hours of the night he found it hard to sleep; his bed had never seemed so empty.

In the morning at breakfast, he told Jenny about a decision he had made. "As far as my new job will let me," he said, "I'm going to live on my station for a while. I've never been an outdoorsman, but Jack can teach me the things about the business I need to know."

She gave him her warm approval. "Louise and I talked about it, and we agreed that it's the logical thing for you to do. Unless you plan to go back home permanently."

"I don't think I could do that now," he told her. "I've got too much of a stake here, and I don't want to give it up."

They sat very close together on the jam-packed flight to Queenstown, but that was by necessity. When they were in the terminal, he tried to defer their parting. "How about dinner tonight?" he asked.

"I'm sorry," Jenny answered. "But we're back just in time for me to keep a long-standing date with Chuck O'Malley, Ray's son. I told you about him."

"Yes, you did," he acknowledged. Quite suddenly he found himself hating a man he had never met, but there was nothing he could do about it at the moment. He looked toward the entrance and saw Louise McHugh coming toward them. She was wearing a pair of regular jeans and a checkered shirt tucked in at the waist. Plain as her outfit was, it accentuated her good figure and the easy way she walked.

She greeted Jenny and then turned to Peter. "Welcome back," she said. "I've got a car waiting. Unless you want to stop in town first, we can go right out to the station."

"I may have some mail at the Mountaineer."

"I picked it up on the way; it's in the car."

As he went to claim his checked luggage, he wondered how she had remembered to get his mail. Then the thought of Jenny being with another man again crowded his mind.

Bag in hand, he turned to go to her once more, to at least tell her how much he had enjoyed her company. Understatement, he decided, might be the best way.

She was standing halfway across the terminal talking to a man who had clearly come to meet her. He was in his late twenties, six feet or more, firmly built, and—Peter faced it—remarkably handsome, despite the fact that he was leaning on a cane. It would be impossibly awkward to try to speak to her, so he turned and went out to the car.

He put his bag inside on the back seat and then held the door open for Louise. As she climbed in, he was glad that he would not have to make the drive back to the station alone. Louise would be good company, and at that point, he needed it.

C H A P T E R   28

As soon as they reached the end of Queenstown, the warmth and clarity of the day began to work their magic. The open vistas of New Zealand offered a compelling invitation to be part of the vast beauty displayed before them: open fields, serene mountains, and the brilliant blue water of the lake. Peter took it all in and then asked, "Do you enjoy living here?"

"Oh, yes!" Louise answered.

There was no need for her to add to that. Peter glanced at her a moment, then wondered how people ever become entrapped in the misery of urban blight. Perhaps it was their karma and they had no choice.

"Did you have a nice time on your tour?" Louise asked. It was a simple question, but it could be pregnant with nuance if he chose to take it that way.

"Yes, I did. I didn't expect to see Jenny—that was quite a surprise." He thought carefully and then said, "She added a lot to the trip."

"Of course she would. She's a very lovely girl—in every way."

He sensed that it was time to change the subject. "Where do you spend most of your time—at the station?"

"Our station, yes. During the tourist season, I help out here and there in town, but mostly I work at home. There's always a lot to do."

"I know your father; tell me about the rest of your family."

"I'm it," Louise replied. "Mother died some time ago, and I'm the only sprout. Dad and I are pretty much pals. He really wanted a son, but I do the best that I can."

"I can't believe he was disappointed," Peter said. "I like you very much as you are."

"Thank you for saying so. Are you going to stay here, Peter?" she asked.

"Yes," he answered. "Will you help me with all the things I have to learn?"

"If you want me to."

He drove on, sorting out his thoughts, until Louise showed him where to turn off onto a well-maintained dirt road. A few minutes later, he pulled up before the big, rambling ranch house that was now his home.

As he got out of the car, Jack McHugh came to greet him. He shook hands with a firm grip and then reached into the car for the luggage. "Come in, Peter," he said. "Tea will be ready as soon as you are. And there's a message for you. You're to call a Mr. Swarthmore in the States. He said you have the number."

That called for immediate action. He went to the telephone in the large living room, raised the operator, and put through the call. In a surprisingly short time Charlie Swarthmore was on the line.

"Peter, how are you?" he asked.

"Fine, just fine."

"I've got very good news for you. You came through. I have a very nice letter from Mr. Bishop enclosing his proxy. That seals it—there's no way Pricane can take us over now."

"Wonderful," Peter said.

"Now, I've heard about the property you inherited from your mother's estate. What are you going to do about this?"

"Charlie, I'm not sure yet. I may divide my time between S and S and my station here. Can you give me a few more days?"

"I'll give you a whole damned year if you want it. Just let me know when to expect you."

"Good enough, thank you," Peter said. "I'll keep you in the picture."

"I was glad when I heard that you were boning up on station management at the library," Jack said during lunch. "I knew then that you were going to come and stay here, at least for a while."

Louise added to that. "You see, we had a fear that when you finally turned up, you might take a quick look at the station and then put it up for sale. You know there's a foreign group that wants to buy it right now."

Peter nodded. "As I told you, I'm not selling. This is my home now. Just don't leave me here alone with no experience in running a place like this."

"You're safe enough in that," Jack assured him. "But you can see why we've been worried. The whole area around here is nice and peaceful; we want to keep it that way."

Peter finished his sandwich and reached for another. "When can I start work?" he asked.

"How about your job with the tourism people?"

"I was told to come here and stay until they send for me." Peter glanced at his watch. "I think it would be a good idea to check in with them."

Following the instructions he had been given, Peter placed a call to the office of the Honorable Warren Cooper. When he mentioned his name, the secretary on the line put him through to the minister personally.

"Good afternoon, Peter," Cooper greeted him. "How are things going?"

"That's what I called to report, sir. While we were at the Bay of Islands, I received a message from Superintendent Winston. He recommended that my companion and I leave there and that I come here to my station. I took that to be an official directive; I hope I did right."

"No doubt, Peter. You've probably heard that two of the Australian gang we have been after are now in custody. We don't know at present where the other three are. Since dealing with them is strictly a police matter, we felt it would be best to keep you out of the way until it's concluded."

"What are your instructions, sir."

"Stay right where you are until we contact you. By the way,

you seem to have made a good friend up north, Constable Pettibone. He speaks highly of you. When we next meet, I'll want to hear about your encounter with Mr. Kincaid."

Peter replaced the phone with a tinge of regret, but Cooper had been right—it was a job for the police and one they were trained to handle. He went back to the kitchen and reported the gist of the conversation to the McHughs.

"Not to worry," Jack told him. "You'll need the time to get used to the station."

To start things off, Louise took him on a detailed tour of the house. They went first to a huge attic where a variety of things, decades old, had been carefully stored. There were many impressive rooms in the house, all of them well furnished and maintained.

Back in the big, airy living room Jack added some more details. "We have to be careful of fire here. A while ago the house at Walter Peak Station burned down and they had to build a whole new one—not as good as the first. Because we're so much on our own here, I spent some money to put in a protection system. There's a new tank up above that will supply plenty of water by gravity feed, so we aren't dependent on pumps, though there's a good one on the line if we need a faster flow. There's a large-size tap in front of the house and two in back. Tomorrow I'll show you how the whole system operates. I put a good extinguisher in the kitchen and one on the first floor—that's the second floor to you. Do you smoke, Peter?"

"No, I don't."

"That's a blessing, because lots of fires start that way."

"What other protective systems do we have?"

"That's about it—fire is our main concern. We don't have any trouble with thieves, not in these parts."

Peter excused himself and went to his room. He stretched himself across the big bed with the intention of taking just a few minutes rest. He awoke when he discovered that Louise was shaking his shoulder. "Dinner's ready," she said.

He went to the kitchen to discover that the meal was being served in the formal dining room. "Do you always go to this much bother?" he asked as he took his place.

"Not usually," Jack answered. "But Louise thought it would be nice tonight—your homecoming and all. After we eat and talk awhile, we'll go to the pub if you'd like."

In four days' time Peter was living in a new world. His station had become the focus of most of his waking hours.

The evening at the pub had been thorougly enjoyable. He had met a number of other station men and had liked them all. Despite the fact that he was a foreigner, he had been accepted, largely because he had come with Jack McHugh. Many glasses had been raised and he had drunk a little too much, but for once he did not need to care.

The next morning he had met two more of the hands, Tom and Derek, both sturdy outdoorsmen. They called him Mr. Ferguson, and when he suggested the use of his first name, they declined. "They're good men," Jack explained to him, "well suited to what they're doing. Don't be afraid to be the owner when you're with them, because you are."

On the third day he had taken the Jeep and explored his property on his own. At the top of a considerable hill he discovered another spectacular view of Lake Wakatipu and miles of the surrounding area.

Jack was gone that evening. Since the hands got their own food and preferred it that way, Peter ate in the kitchen with Louise. "Dad is over at our place," she said as a sizable steak was put in front of each of them. "He'll be back in the morning."

"Are you going to stay here tonight?" he asked.

"If you don't mind."

"Don't be absurd," he told her. "This place is yours and Jack's as much as it's mine. You belong here."

In the morning Jack came back in time for breakfast. "I think today, Peter, if you don't have other plans, we ought to go over the station books together," he said. "You should know just where you stand and how well the place is doing."

"Fine," Peter agreed. Seated at the large kitchen table, they were well started when Louise left in the light truck. A few seconds later, a bell rang when she passed over the treadle wire in the roadway that gave advance notice of arriving visitors. The weather warmed rapidly, and the feel of the sun coming through the windows was a touch of unadulterated luxury.

When the time came for lunch, they took it out of doors and ate at a picnic table that stood on the front lawn.

"Now that you've been here a bit, how do you like it?" Jack asked.

Peter looked about him before he answered. He felt the gentle stirring of the air against the side of his face, listened to the bird songs that he had heard so seldom before, and enjoyed the richness of the sun on his back. "It's too good to be true," he answered.

Jack leaned his huge frame forward and put his work-hardened hands together. "It's a pretty good life, Peter. There are many things we don't have, of course, but we live in peace, and that's a lot."

A loud bell rang under the eaves of the ranch house. "That's the phone," Jack said. Peter ran into the kitchen, picked up the instrument there, and said, "Oldshire Station."

"Ray O'Malley, Peter, calling from Wellington. I had a session this morning with the immigration people. The paperwork for your permanent residency is approved and filed. Also, Superintendent Winston sends his regards."

"Was he in on this, too?"

"He did speak a word on your behalf. And don't be worried about your new job. At the moment you're being asked to stay right where you are."

"Any news about the Australians?"

"Nothing I can discuss, but I'm sure that steps are being taken. As soon as they're captured, you'll be notified."

"I hope so," Peter said. "Meanwhile, I'm getting to like this place more every day."

As soon as the conversation was over, Peter phoned his aunt. As he waited for her to come on the line, he was grateful that he had someone who cared enough about him to be concerned with his welfare. As soon as he told her the news, Martha was jubilant. "Peter, that's wonderful!" she burst out. "We've been hoping for this, but we weren't sure how you felt."

153

"You know now," Peter said. "I'll still be an American citizen, but I'm finding some roots here."

"Come and see us very soon," Martha pleaded.

"I will," he promised.

By the end of the day he had discovered that the station was making good money, but it also took a great deal of upkeep. He also learned how careful and astute Jack had been in managing the property.

He knew it would be some time before he would be qualified to cope with it all.

"There's no way I can run this place without you, Jack," he said when they stopped for tea. "If the present arrangement is satisfactory to you, I'd like to keep it going for a while. You teach me, and I'll do my best to learn."

McHugh was pleased. "We'd been hoping, Peter, that if you did turn up, you'd be someone solid. I don't mind carrying on as long as you'd like, and Louise feels the same way. She's done a lot of the work, you know."

As he got ready for dinner, Peter did some thinking. It had just been brought home to him that the entertainments available to station dwellers were very limited. He could see many evenings stretching ahead when he would have little to do but sit and read, or work on the books. He was used to a lifestyle much different from that. Compared to station life, even Queenstown had some conviviality to offer.

As he went to bed, he thought again of Jenny; he would have given a lot to have had her there with him. He tossed and turned until his fatigue took him away and at last he slept.

He half awoke when he thought he heard the sound of a bell ringing. The idea of the telephone entered his mind, but as he sat up, he realized that the ring had not been repeated. At that moment the door of his room was flung open, and Louise ran in. He vaulted out of bed, knowing there was some kind of trouble. "What is it?" he demanded.

Louise didn't waste a moment. "Someone's outside, someone who doesn't belong here."

CHAPTER 29

Wearing only his pajama bottoms, he bent over and as fast as possible began to put on his shoes. Before he could finish that simple operation, Louise was gone.

Wasting no more time, he hurried down the stairs. Just before he reached the main floor he saw, or thought he saw, a leaping tongue of flame. At once he remembered that fire was the greatest danger the station had to face. He grabbed the extinguisher off the wall and reached the kitchen just in time to see Jack going out the door on the run. Peter followed, knowing that the main fire-fighting equipment was all outside. As he burst through the doorway, by the light of an almost full moon he saw at least two other figures, possibly Tom and Derek, the hands who slept in the bunkhouse.

For a bare moment he paused, uncertain what he should do; then he heard the sudden blast of a firearm. He saw the flash of a gun on the other side of the lawn, then the massive figure of Jack McHugh crumpling to the ground.

The reflexes that he had once trained and sharpened took hold. He threw the extinguisher aside and with a burst of controlled energy hurled himself forward in a flat-out sprint. The dim figure of a man aimed a gun at him; he instantly jerked himself sideways. He saw the flash of the shot before he registered the blast of sound. Dodging and weaving as he ran, in four desperate seconds he covered all but the last few feet that separated him from the gunman. Then he hurled his body forward with his arms outstretched. A third shot blasted his eardrums, but his mind was totally locked on the thing he was doing. His bare shoulders smashed against the gunman's legs; as the man went down under him, a burst of savage satisfaction told him his tackle had been close to perfect. The gunman was big and heavily dressed, but that was no matter. Peter knew he had hit him as hard as anyone could be hit on a football field.

The moment they slammed against the ground Peter released his hold, jumped up, and kicked the gunman's right wrist as hard as he could. He made solid contact—the man screamed and dropped his weapon. As Peter dove for it, he heard another shot, and the biting zing of a bullet barely missed his ear.

He looked up and saw another man, forty feet away, pointing a gun at him with a two-handed grip.

As he saw the barrel held in position, he knew instantly that his life was over. He dropped down and tried again to grab the gun, hoping to last long enough to get off at least one answering round; then the sound of another shot surrounded him.

For a second or two he felt nothing. He knew it was the anesthesia of shock—the momentary holding off of pain while the body accepts the fact that it has been traumatically injured. He grasped the gun, looked toward his killer to take aim if he could, and saw the man beginning to pitch forward. He swung his head toward the sound of the shot and saw Louise standing in the doorway with a rifle locked against her shoulder. Then he knew she had just saved his life.

The man lying beside him jerked out a hand and grabbed for the gun. Peter was caught by surprise, but his body was fully charged and he reacted almost instantaneously. From his crouched position he kicked his opponent with maximum force in the side just below the kidney. As his shoe rammed home, at the side limit of his vision he saw Jack McHugh try to get up and then fall back again.

The firelight was glowing brighter. A long plume of flame had curled around the corner of the ranch house and was leaping up toward the sky. He wanted to run for the extinguisher he had dropped, but he did not dare to leave the man he had felled.

The unexpected sound of a vehicle stabbed the night as a fresh outburst of flame framed the doorway where Louise had been standing. With a racing engine a car came charging onto the far end of the lawn, its headlights fixed on the form of Jack McHugh as he lay on the ground. Silhouetted by fresh flames that had taken a sudden new spurt behind her, Louise swung her rifle to her shoulder and fired again.

The car began to drift to the right, its headlights picking a new path. Slowly the rate of the turn increased, away from where Jack lay, until the vehicle passed him by a good fifteen feet. With its rate of turn still increasing, it almost reached the end of the lawn, where a huge old tree loomed in its way. The car hit it head on

156

with a crashing impact. The hood flew up and back as the whole vehicle seemed to fold like an accordian. For a moment the rear end lifted of the ground, then fell back down. The engine was abruptly still. Within a few seconds there was a popping sound, a sudden acrid odor, and the whole vehicle burst into flames.

Peter looked toward the man who had tried to kill him and saw him lying motionless on the grass. His prisoner at his feet was also still. The kick in the side could have driven most of the wind out of his body, but this was no time to take chances. Over the rising crackling of the flames that were spreading down the whole side of the house, he shouted to Louise, "Come here!"

She heard him and came running, her rifle in her hands. When she reached him, he pointed to the man on the ground. "Hold him!"

Louise backed up a few steps and held her rifle at the ready so that if the prisoner tried to get up, he would find himself looking straight down the barrel.

The moment he was free, Peter ran to Jack McHugh. The big man lay on his back breathing heavily, his face tightened in pain. Peter knelt beside him and tried to make himself understood. "Take it easy, Jack—we got them. I'll get some help."

He took off toward the house, where Derek and Tom, in shoes and night clothing, had a good-size hose working; Derek was directing the water at the hottest spots while Tom was digging up huge shovelfuls of turf from the lawn and throwing them at the base of the flames. As Peter ran up, Tom shouted, "Firebomb—gasoline," while he threw another shovelful where it would be most effective.

"Andy?" Peter asked.

"In town."

Peter lowered his head, took a deep breath, and charged through the flaming doorway. He ran for the telephone, desperately hoping it would still be working. He dialed the operator; when she responded he used as few words as possible. "This is Oldshire Station. We've been attacked and are on fire. Jack McHugh, the manager, has been shot. We need help, a doctor, and the police."

"Right away," the operator said, her voice crisp and clear.

Peter hung up and ran back to where the flames were still flooding the side of the house.

Both Tom and Derek knew what they were doing. Derek was using a hose. Tom was working like a madman spading up soil from the lawn and flinging it onto what remained of the burning fuel.

From the fire rack Peter seized another spade to help, but the first time he thrust the tool into the ground, his right shoulder burned with a fire of its own and he was forced to stop; he could endure no more. Staying on his feet with an effort, he went to Louise and took the rifle from her. "Look after Jack," he said.

He saw Louise run to her father and kneel down beside him. Because his own pain was pounding relentlessly, he was grateful to be standing still. The man on the ground moved occasionally, but he made no attempt to get to his feet.

Another pair of headlights came into view, a truck stopped, and four men jumped out to help. After that it was much easier. Peter's shoulder had frozen into position; he could not move it at all. For the first time he wondered if it was broken.

To his left a light came on in the sky, and the sound of a helicopter grew rapidly in volume. Visibility had to be poor even in the bright moonlight, but with his landing light the pilot put the machine down smoothly on the far edge of the lawn.

Louise appeared beside him. "That'll be the doctor," she said. "You'd better meet him."

Peter gave her back her rifle and ran toward the machine. The doctor lost no time in getting out. He was a big, burly man and bearded, with the authority of his profession surrounding him. Peter had never met him, but that didn't matter. "Jack McHugh's been shot," he said. "He's lying there on the lawn—we didn't try to move him."

"You did right. Any others?"

"Two of the three who attacked us. They may be dead; Louise shot them with a rifle."

"She isn't likely to have missed," the doctor said. Bag in hand, he hurried to look after Jack.

In a moment or two Peter felt his tension begin to lessen. The fire was virtually out, and there was expert help on hand. Since he could do nothing more there, he went back to where Louise was standing guard over the prisoner. "I'll take over," he told her, and held out his left hand for the rifle.

"No," Louise said. "Leave him to me." Her tone was not vengeful, but the man she was watching had shot her father.

From inside the house the sound of the alarm bell came once more. Shortly a police car, its blue roof light rotating, came in and stopped. Sergeant Bill Woodley was first out, followed by two uniformed constables. Woodley took in the whole scene with one sweeping glance as Peter came to meet him. "We got a 'most urgent' from the telephone operator," he said. "What happened, briefly?"

"Three men attacked the station sometime after midnight. They set fire to the house, and when Jack came running out, they shot him."

"Did you see that?"

"Yes. Louise shot one of them when he tried to kill me. Another one of them came charging across the lawn in a car, trying to hit Jack. She shot him, too."

Woodley nodded toward the silent wreck. "That's the car, I take it."

"Yes. There's a man on the south end of the lawn where Louise dropped him, dead or injured. Another one in the car."

Without using words, Woodley gestured to one of the constables to check out the man lying on the grass. The second he sent to inspect the car.

"And the one Louise is holding?"

"That's the man who shot Jack. When I saw Jack go down, I took him out."

"How?"

"With an open field tackle."

"Could you see that the man you faced had a gun?"

"I didn't have to."

"Of course. Then what did you do?"

"I went after him. He took a shot at me but missed when I went into a broken field pattern. As soon as I was close enough, I made a diving tackle and took him down."

"You're a football player?"

"Yes."

The first constable came up to report. "He's dead, sergeant. I'll ask the doctor to confirm it, but he took a bullet right through the heart."

The other constable, looking slightly sick, came from the opposite direction. "There's a corpse in the car," he said. "Not pretty—badly burned."

"Any chance he's still alive?"

"None. The body's pretty far gone." He took a deep breath. "Do you want me to get him out?"

Instead of answering, Woodley went across the lawn to where the doctor was still working over the big form of Jack McHugh. "How about it?" he asked.

The doctor shook his head. "I've got to get him into hospital as soon as possible. I'm trying to stabilize him first, but it's proving difficult."

"If you can rig a litter, I'll take him," the pilot volunteered.

"Thanks, Mark," the doctor answered. "I'll fix something."

Peter went quickly to where Tom and Derek were waiting with the four men who had come to help. "We need a litter for Jack," he said. "One that can fit in the helicopter. Have we got anything?"

"Yes, Mr. Ferguson, we've got most things we might need," Derek answered. As he and Tom went for the litter, Peter returned to where Jack was lying. "They're bringing something," he said.

The doctor merely nodded. He lifted a plastic container and spoke to one of the constables, who was intently watching. "Here, hold this."

Peter looked again toward Louise and saw that Woodley and the other constable had taken the prisoner in charge. The man was protesting loudly in a thick accent, "Keep those damned cuffs off me—me bleedin' arm's broken!"

"We'll have the doctor look at you—when he's finished elsewhere," Woodley said. "Meanwhile, you're under arrest: attempted murder and arson. More charges to be added later." He turned his flashlight into the man's face. "Edward Riley," he said. "I've seen your photo often enough."

After searching the prisoner for possible additional weapons, he gave instructions. "Hold him here until the doctor's free to

160

look at his arm. Don't talk to him, and don't let him move one foot off this spot."

That done, he went to where Peter was standing and dropped a hand on his bare shoulder. "You showed some good form tonight," he began then stopped abruptly when Peter could not avoid a sharp wince of pain. "What happened to your shoulder?" he asked.

"The tackle. I him him pretty hard."

"We'll have the doctor look at that. Stay here while I speak to him."

At that moment Tom hurried up with a canvas litter. Under the doctor's supervision Jack was carefully lifted onto it and carried over to the helicopter. The senior constable walked alongside, holding up the solution bottle and the tube that led down to Jack's arm. It took some time to put the litter into the machine in a safe and reasonably comfortable position. Jack's bulk made things much more difficult, but as soon as the problem had been solved, the pilot started the engine and lifted off in less than a minute.

As the helicopter climbed and turned toward Queenstown, the senior constable took over the duty of guarding Riley. Woodley spoke to the doctor, who came over at once to Peter. "I'll have a look at that shoulder now," he declared. With his fingers he explored carefully and with surprising gentleness, keeping the necessary added pain to a minimum. "You've got a fracture there, my lad," he said. "I've got to call the hospital about Jack. I want you there too for X-rays. Get some clothes on if you can; if not, wrap yourself in a blanket."

"I'll look after him," Louise said. Leaving Peter no room for argument, she led the way into the house.

When Peter went outside again, he found that the first hints of dawn were in the sky. The alarm bell rang once more, and an ambulance unit came rolling in. The doctor strode briskly toward the vehicle and spoke to the two men inside. "We have two deceased," he said. "I've verified that. One is pretty messy; he burned up in a car wreck. You'll have to get him out."

"We've done it before," the driver said, and opened the door.

The doctor took advantage of a few free moments to speak to Peter. "In a situation of this kind, I have to see to the most se-

161

verely injured first. The look of the car told me that anyone inside had to be dead. There would be no living through that blaze. If Louise had shot him, then he was almost certainly dead before the car hit the tree."

"She's good with a rifle," Peter said.

"You can believe that, even in a bad light. Now I have to see to the prisoner, although I doubt his arm's broken."

As soon as the doctor had left, Tom came to report to Peter.

"There's some damage, but not so bad it can't be fixed," he said. "You'll need to get a carpenter in, but mostly we got to the fire in time. The water system cost, but without it you'd have lost the lot, and no mistake."

Peter thanked him and went into the house, where the doctor was phoning. He looked out the window and saw that the ambulance men were removing the body from the burned out car. The police, with Riley in custody, had already left. So had the four men who had come to help.

Louise came into the room. "Let's have a quick cuppa before we leave for Queenstown," she said. As she went toward the kitchen, he watched the way she carried herself. She had killed two men during the night just past, but not a hint of it showed in her bearing.

When the telephone rang, Peter's heart jumped; he was very afraid that it would be bad news about Jack. "Oldshire Station," he answered.

"Is that you, Peter? Winston here. I'm told you've just had quite a do."

"Yes," Peter answered, his voice thick with relief.

"Is everything under control, as you say?"

"Jack McHugh, my manager, has been shot."

Winston's voice almost leaped over the wire. "How badly?"

"I don't know yet. He was taken to the hospital by helicopter; he should be there now."

"Any other casualties?"

"Two of the men who attacked us are dead. The third is in custody."

"So I've heard. We wanted him very much."

"Sergeant Woodley did a fine job, by the way."

162

"Expected of him, but glad to hear it." There was a pause, then Winston spoke again. "Peter, I won't keep you now, but we must talk very soon. I don't understand this at all."

Louise came to the doorway, holding a cup of tea. Peter nodded. "I think I do," he said.

CHAPTER 30

As the Boeing 737 of Air New Zealand approached the channel that separates the South and North Island, the air began to become very rough. It was almost always that way, due to the ventura effect of the narrow passage. Although several days had passed since the attack, Peter gritted his teeth and endured the agony that each sharp bump inflicted on his broken shoulder. Fortunately, it was soon over, and the compact airliner came down for a smooth landing at the Wellington airport.

Ray O'Malley was there to meet him. "It's all confirmed," he said. "We're meeting with the Honorable Warren Cooper at his office. We've plenty of time, so don't worry about that."

"Do you know what he has in mind?" Peter asked.

"I expect it will have to do with the recent attempts of some outside interests to interfere with our tourist industry. However, there's something else I want to discuss with you, Peter."

From the tone of his voice it struck Peter that it would be bad news. "Jack McHugh?" he asked.

"No, he's coming along fine, the last I heard."

Inwardly, Peter braced himself for whatever Ray had to tell him "Go ahead," he said.

"It concerns Jenny, Peter. I've known her since she was a little girl. She and my son pretty much grew up together."

Peter sensed what was coming, and a sharp stab of pain seemed to fill his whole body.

"For some time we expected that eventually they'd be married, but an accident to my son put everything on hold."

"I heard about it," Peter said. "Jenny told me."

O'Malley negotiated a traffic circle as he headed on into Wellington. "When you appeared on the scene, Peter, she liked you very much. Then when you both came back from the Bay of Islands, my son met her at the airport. Later that evening, he asked her if she would marry him. She didn't give him an immediate answer; instead, she went to Christchurch and spent a week there to think things over. When she came back two days ago, she gave him a yes answer. She wanted to tell you about this herself, but there was no good way to do that. So I offered to do it for her."

Peter found it hard to shape the right words, but he managed to say, "Thank you very much."

O'Malley changed his tone and became more calmly factual. "I know you like her and that she likes you, but your total time together has been only a few days. You understand what I'm saying."

"Yes, I do," Peter answered. "She's a remarkably attractive girl, but as you say, we've hardly gotten to know one another. Seriously, that is."

"Good for you, Peter. I admire you for that. I hope that nothing will stand in the way of the three of you becoming very good friends."

"Of course not," Peter answered, but his heart was not in his words. He was glad that they were already close to the center of Wellington, where other thoughts would necessarily take over his mind.

Ray parked the car and led the way into a modern, impressive office building. Fortunately, the elevator they took was almost empty, and no one jostled his arm for a change.

When the car stopped and the door opened, they stepped out into a reception area. The first thing Peter saw was Kincaid, taking his ease in a comfortable chair and reading an Australian magazine.

"Minister Cooper will be with you shortly, gentlemen," the receptionist said. "Meanwhile, can I get you some refreshments?"

O'Malley politely declined with a gesture. "Is Superintendent Winston here yet?" he asked.

"Yes, he's in with Mr. Cooper now."

Less than five minutes later she picked up the ringing phone on her desk and spoke briefly. Then she got easily to her feet and led them across the reception area to Minister Cooper's office. She opened the door and showed them inside. Cooper was standing, waiting for them, with Winston at his side. "Good morning, gentlemen," he said. "I presume you've all met."

Peter realized that wasn't the case. He turned to his two companions and swiftly corrected the omission. "Mr. O'Malley, Mr. Kincaid," he said.

"Pleased to meet you, counselor." Kincaid was pleasantly cordial, but Peter was once again annoyed that the Pricane executive knew so much about his private business. As if on cue Kincaid turned to Peter. "How is your shoulder?" he asked.

The same thing again. "Better, thanks," Peter answered. He was annoyed with himself that he had been a touch too abrupt: it automatically made Kincaid look a little taller in the saddle.

"Please sit down," the minister said. "I'll have some tea brought in, and then we can discuss certain matters."

A young woman carrying a formal tea service appeared within seconds. After the ritual of distribution had been observed, Warren took the floor.

"I've been very concerned about several recent events, most of which have to do with our tourist industry. Peter, I've heard, of course, about the attack on your station and the splendid way that you defended yourselves. Now all five of the Australian villains we were after have been dealt with. Two of them are dead and three are in custody, including the most wanted man of all. So I venture to hope that this unfortunate episode is now concluded."

The simple thing at that point would have been to agree with the minister, but Peter's mind was too sharply focused on the topic for that. "I think, sir," he said, "that while this individual episode may be closed, as you say, it doesn't conclude the matter. I have reason to believe that a very sticky patch, as I believe you say, is in front of us all."

The Honorable Warren Cooper looked at Winston, then back to Peter. "That's quite a startling statement," he said. "I would certainly like to hear whatever you have to tell us."

It was put up or shut up time, and Peter was ready. He had planned very carefully just what he was going to say.

"Not long after I came to New Zealand, I became involved in a series of events that didn't appear to make any sense. The more I thought about them, the less I could understand them.

"At first I accepted the idea that some Australian hard types had been sent here by a Hong Kong syndicate to muscle in on the tourist industry. Superficially, that explanation seemed to fit the visible facts. It could also account for the attack on my station. Before I took over, they had pressed Jack McHugh to sell it to them even though he didn't have the title."

"I didn't know that," Winston said.

Peter continued. "During the first day or two after I hurt my shoulder, I had to stay inactive. That gave me time to think. I asked myself a number of questions. Why would anybody deliberately throw a body onto the hood of my car? Why was a policeman assaulted for no visible reason? Why was Mr. MacTavish murdered at Russell just before we arrived there? Most of all, what was the real reason that my place was attacked and Jack McHugh, my manager, gunned down?

"These looked like a series of terrorist activities intended to frighten people into selling. The burning down of the pub supported that idea; the owner had refused an offer, and he was put out of business a few days later. It might even explain the murder of Ned MacTavish, who also had refused to sell his property. But it didn't account for the attack on Constable Fisher or for throwing a body onto my car. More than that, if the men doing all this were professionals, then why were they going about it in a totally wrong way?

"Terrorist actions may frighten some people, but much more often they only make them mad. Even if I wanted to sell my property, I would never let it go to people who tried to burn me out and who nearly killed both me and my manager. I'd be dead right now except for the fact that Jack McHugh's daughter is a crack shot with a rifle.

"As I thought it out, one point in particular came to me. What if I had been killed? It would have thrown my estate—which means the station—back into the courts. No one would have

166

been able to buy it until all the legal questions had been settled. That, combined with several other things, convinced me that the 'muscle-in' theory wouldn't work."

Minister Cooper nodded his acceptance of that, then said, "Go ahead, please."

"Next, I thought about Pricane. It's a ruthless organization; Mr. Kincaid said so himself. It buys a lot of political clout. Public officials who are in the way are bypassed or maneuvered out of office. Recently, it's been publicized that Pricane has been passing out substantial sums under the table both at home and abroad. For several years it's been building an image of invincibility; if Pricane was coming after you, the best you could do was to grab any deal you could get and run for the exit. So far, would you say that I'm being accurate, Mr. Kincaid?"

Kincaid was caught unaware, but he recovered quickly.

"Substantially, yes. The nature of conglomerates is well known."

"Because of all this, I thought it possible that through the Hong Kong group the Australian terrorists were actually working for Pricane. Using straw men—people not known to be part of the organization—has been a favorite Pricane tactic for years.

"But there are two substantial objections that throw this theory out the window. Pricane has been relentless in some of its manipulations, and it's done many things that were illegal, but it's never been known to resort to murder. This isn't so much ethics as practicality. If the company were to be caught in anything like that, its stock would go down ten points in one day."

The minister looked at Kincaid. "Do you still agree with him to this point?" he asked.

This time Kincaid was ready. "What he has said has been in published reports." It was a neat way of deflating Peter, and everyone present knew it.

"In reputable media?"

"Yes, sir," Kincaid answered. "We've entered suit."

"I expect that you would," the minister commented. "Please go on, Peter."

"The second reason why blaming Pricane won't hold water is the fact that the company is under congressional investigation.

167

Legally, it's walking on eggshells at the moment, so it's no time to try any kind of questionable tactics. Pricane has been pulling in its horns as fast as it can."

Kincaid leaned forward to take the floor. "For the record," he said, "Ferguson is right about Pricane's non-involvement in the violence here. I'm in charge of our New Zealand activities. For both business and ethical reasons, I wouldn't condone anything like that for a moment. You have my word on it."

"Accepted," the minister said.

Peter hitched his chair forward an inch or so, just to give his muscles a little exercise. "Now comes something that gave me an important clue. I told you that my companion and I arrived at the Bay of Islands just after a local resident had been murdered. His name was Ned MacTavish. He owned a small piece of property at a prime site, one badly wanted by developers to put up a large hotel. Mr. MacTavish was pressed to sell, but he refused. Then Mr. Kincaid tried to buy an option on the property, without success. I was there at the time."

Peter glanced at Kincaid, but the Pricane executive was maintaining his role as a dispassionate listener.

"Murdering the owner would be no way to convince his widow to sell out to his suspected killers. Also, there was bound to be a backlash of public outrage, particularly in a very small community where MacTavish was well known and respected. That's a powerful force, and no one in his right mind would go against it.

"I knew that MacTavish was well off, but I didn't know how he got his money or what work he'd done. So I phoned a man who I knew would have the answers, if he would give them to me."

"Constable Pettibone," Winston said.

"Yes. Since the information wasn't confidential, he answered my question. First, MacTavish had inherited some money, and so had his wife. He was astute in his business dealings and had increased his holdings substantially. The second answer gave me a key piece of information."

Peter was human enough to pause a moment for effect. "Before he retired, Mr. MacTavish was a high-ranking policeman."

168

Minister Cooper looked at Superintendent Winston. "I hadn't been told that," he said.

"It's correct, sir. It's well known in Russell and certain other places, but in this instance we thought it best not to advertise."

"I see. Go on, Peter."

Peter did. "That's all I have to say about Pricane. Next comes the Hong Kong group. Apart from the fact that it exists and that it has very substantial financial resources, I know almost nothing about it. But if it has been so successful, then it's a good assumption that it's made up of astute businessmen—astute enough to know better than to let their agents kill an undercover policeman, violently attack another, burn down a property they're trying to buy, and then murder a property owner in cold blood. After such actions, what possible hope would they have of successfully going into business here? The kiwis I've met aren't the kind of people to give in to anything like that."

"I trust not," the minister said.

"Now I'd like to ask Superintendent Winston some questions," Peter said. "Going back to the incident of the murdered police officer who was thrown onto the hood of my car: how much investigative work has gone into that matter?"

"A great deal," Winston answered.

"And the attack on the constable on patrol—I don't recall his name."

"Fred Fisher. Same answer."

"The burning down of the pub?"

"Not as much, because we were pretty sure who did it. Also, we were heavily overloaded at the time."

"Lastly, how much of a spoor did you pick up from the Hong Kong group?"

"Peter, I'll ask you to withdraw that question for the moment."

That was a setback to Peter's plan of presentation, but he accepted it. "Then let me say this: I know these people have hired a reputable real estate agent to negotiate purchases for them, and that's it. So unless there is some provable connection between

169

the Australians and the Hong Kong people, they should be out of it as far as police interests are concerned."

"That's eminently logical," Winston said, "but I have to interject something here. You may take it as given that the Australian villains *are* connected with the Hong Kong people."

"Then some of what I have to say isn't valid," Peter declared.

"I still want to hear it," the minister said.

"I'm about to suggest something that as far as I know hasn't come up before—that the Australian villains, as you call them, have been acting on their own."

"To what purpose?" O'Malley asked.

"Let me put it this way: those men came here and took some very dangerous chances, even with the unarmed police. They did things that seemed to be associated with the tourist industry, but some of their actions were definitely not. The attack on Constable Fisher, for example. I couldn't reconcile what they were doing with any kind of planned industrial campaign. That particularly pertains to highly visible murder, such as throwing a body onto my car. I don't doubt that people have been done away in business as well as politics, but not so blatantly, and that may be the key to the whole thing."

"What were they up to, then?" the minister asked.

"I believe, sir, they were deliberately making the biggest waves they could to keep the police overcommitted and off balance. The force has only so much manpower and resources. According to what Winston just told us, they succeeded in tying up a large portion of what's available.

"I doubt that the Australians are really interested in any real estate here. It's too often a long-term proposition, and real estate transactions are usually subject to some kind of official scrutiny. But I've heard that Edward Riley, who's in custody, has heavy connections in the narcotics trade. It's no secret that there are huge profits possible in that business, with a fast turnover. In view of what Winston just said, the people in Hong Kong could be Riley's source of supply.

"In the United States there are thousands of possible places to cross our borders, legally or otherwise, but that isn't true here. Light planes can't fly in and out, because they don't have the range. Most of the pleasure boats I've seen haven't got ocean-going capability. The few that do are fairly conspicuous and I presume can be tracked by radar. Going by air or water are the only two ways of getting either into or out of New Zealand.

"When we were at the Bay of Islands," Peter continued, "I couldn't help noticing how many boats of various kinds were gathered there. Russell is a small place and has only one policeman—granted, a very good one. It occurred to me that if someone wanted to do any smuggling in or out of the country, that would be an ideal place.

"All that didn't add up to a lot until I learned that Mr. MacTavish had been a senior police officer. He would be a skilled observer, and his home was located where he had a panoramic view of the whole area. That would make him a serious obstacle to any kind of smuggling operation. I think that's why he was killed."

When Peter stopped, the whole room remained quiet. As the seconds ticked away, he wondered if he had overreached himself. Then Winston broke the silence. "Did you convey any of these ideas to Constable Pettibone?" he asked.

"No," Peter answered, "because I hadn't thought it out until I was back home again. Then it occurred to me that the Australians we've been talking about could be keeping the police seriously overloaded to cover the setting up of a major drug operation. To them, New Zealand might look like a ripe new territory."

"It would explain the murder of MacTavish," the minister noted. "I agree that it didn't make sense otherwise."

"That's all I have to say," Peter concluded.

The minister looked toward Kincaid. "I'd like to know if Pricane is still interested in our tourist industry."

Kincaid replied almost at once. "Yes, particularly if we can work out some sort of a cooperative agreement. We can be of major help. Without offense, your industry is pathetically underdeveloped and inefficient. You're giving people far too much for their money—more than they expect and at prices that could be substantially increased with very little loss of patronage."

"We rather like it as it is," Cooper said. "And financially we do well enough."

"Yes," Kincaid retorted, "but you can't stay in the business dark ages forever. Sooner or later a more aggressive and efficient organization is going to come along and go after the rich potential profits that you're losing every day."

The minister rose to his feet to signal that the meeting was over. "We've been given quite a lot to think about," he said. "I'm most grateful that you all took the time to come."

"Thank you," Peter acknowledged. He knew he had done his best and that it all hadn't come off too badly. As he turned to leave, Winston touched his shoulder. "A few words with you, Peter, if you have the time. Wait for me outside."

Peter did as directed. When Winston emerged, he had Kincaid with him. "I know a place where the three of us can have a quiet coffee together," the superintendent said. "There are some things I think you both should now be told."

In a pleasant, close-by coffee house, Winston, Peter, and Kincaid seated themselves around a table. The atmosphere was far from relaxed, but Winston ignored that. No one else was nearby, which gave them the privacy they needed.

The superintendent took it upon himself to order coffee for everyone. That done, he turned to Kincaid.

"You and Peter have now seen something of our country and the extent of it, but all of our people together couldn't fill up half of New York. Because we don't have the slums and the ghettos that are found in many of your cities, we have had only a limited drug problem in the past. PCP is so far unknown here, but we have set up a careful control of the chemicals used to make it." He folded his hands and put them on the table. "You see, it isn't only a question of the law—it's what illegal drugs could do to our people. I toured an addict treatment center in Hong Kong a short while ago. It wasn't pleasant. Many of the patients were adults and young people from the better levels of society. Drug abuse had reduced them to something less than human.

"Peter, you gave a good analysis of the whole situation, particularly the bit about Chief Superintendent MacTavish. You missed a few things, but your thinking was sound nonetheless."

Winston took some coffee.

"Now, Ted, you assured the minister this morning that Pri-

172

cane had nothing whatever to do with the Hong Kong group. Peter, do you accept that?"

"Not entirely."

Kincaid closed his hands into fists as anger rapidly grew within him. "Why do you doubt my word?" he demanded.

Peter kept his cool. "Because of something you told me when we met outside the MacTavish home. You were talking about the way Pricane always wins; then suddenly you switched and said something like, 'We control a lot of politicians, but we don't hire hit men. Don't blame MacTavish on us.' It was way out of context. Then you went on telling how the tourist business here was going to be a Pricane division."

Kincaid eyed him with hostile sharpness. "You thought I was protesting too much, is that it?"

"It seemed that way."

"Gentlemen," Winston intervened, "my thought is this: when you made your statement this morning, Ted, you spoke the truth as far as you knew. I accept that. At the same time, knowing how Pricane operates, you held open a mental reservation, just in case."

Kincaid partially simmered down. "That's true," he admitted.

"You know a Mr. Lloyd, I believe."

"He's a vice president of Pricane. I report to him."

"Tell me, how recently have you been in touch with your office at home?"

"Not for the last two days. I've been evaluating some property in Nelson. I know there's a major housecleaning going on because of the investigation. What about Lloyd?"

"He was called to testify before a congressional investigation. He refused to answer questions and was found in contempt."

"If he didn't want to talk, he wouldn't," Kincaid said. "He'll get out of it somehow."

"Possibly. Meanwhile, some stockholders of Swarthmore and Stone entered a multimillion dollar suit against Pricane, charging that their proxies were solicited by improper, false, and deceptive means. They have good grounds, I understand."

"That was a week ago," Kincaid said. "I know all about it."

A gentle smile wreathed Winston's features, as if he were a kindly uncle come to dinner with presents for all the kiddies. "Then, Ted, did you also know that yesterday Pricane signed an agreement to cease and desist from any further attempted take-over of Swarthmore and Stone in return for a dismissal of the suit? It had come at such an awkward time, you see."

Kincaid's expression froze; he stared straight ahead, as though in the bright light of day he had suddenly seen an unexpected and foreboding ghost. Small beads of sweat began to break out on his forehead.

Winston returned to his coffee and waited for his victim to speak.

"Since you are so well informed," Kincaid said at last, "where does that leave me?"

"I wouldn't look for any more property here at the moment," Winston replied. "But Swarthmore and Stone may want you to continue as their president."

Kincaid spoke almost mechanically. "There's no chance of that. Actually, I never was the president. I was promised the job, to take effect very shortly. I was to be shoved down their throats. Now Pricane will probably cut mine as fast as they can."

"You're an established Pricane executive with a very good record. Surely, they'll have another place for you."

Kincaid shook his head, forcing himself to face the sudden real-ity. "By Pricane standards, I've let them down. That's fatal. I had nothing to do with those Australians, but that won't matter."

With an effort he regained control of himself. "I gave up a damned good job to come with Pricane—they guaranteed me a vice presidency by next year. But that's history now."

Peter almost felt sorry for him. "It may work out better than you expect," he said.

Kincaid snapped a look at him. "You know about Pricane, so you know that no excuses are ever accepted."

"Whenever Pricane has been in trouble," Peter said, "there's always been a sacrificial lamb to take the fall. Who'll it be this time?"

Kincaid revived a little. "It'll be Lloyd. It will have to be someone high up, and the New Zealand project was his idea. He'll be fed to the wolves in Congress."

The man was still not himself; his smooth, sometimes arrogant manner had entirely deserted him. Carefully he gathered his thoughts together. "You implied that there *is* a connection between Pricane and the Hong Kong people," he said.

Winston nodded. "Yes, that's true. It's a marriage of convenience to give the Hong Kong people a foothold in the United States and Pricane a base for operations in the Far East. That's all I know at the moment."

Peter mercifully changed the topic. "What about the man thrown onto my car?"

"Most tragic," Winston said. "As I told you, he was an undercover officer. We tried to set him up as a New Zealand member of the Australian gang, presumably to help them with local knowledge and contacts. It's obvious they weren't fooled. My guess would be that they convinced him they were going to ambush your car and then lured him up above the road where they dealt with him."

"Why me?"

"You were sent here to do a certain job, and they took advantage of it. We're trying to trace their sources of information, but they knew who you were and that you worked for Swarthmore and Stone."

"Our survey team made some arrangements when it was here," Kincaid said. "That may give you a clue."

It was Winston's turn to be surprised. "Very kind of you to tell us that," he said.

"Self-protection, Superintendent. I don't want to be accused of being an accessory to murder."

Winston nodded. "Very astute of you," he conceded. "I'm sure the evidence, as we gather it, will bear you out. Peter, by throwing the constable's body onto your car, the villains were able to concentrate a great deal of police attention on you and divert it from their own activities. They also showed us how they would treat any other informers. It cost a good man his life. For that they're going to pay dearly."

175

"And the attack on my station?"

"To get you out of the way in a spectacular manner. Unfortunately for them, there was a lady present who is very handy with a rifle. You see, Peter, by demonstrating their supposed power to do things and get away with it, they could impress potential members of their drug network—an old Mafia technique, I believe. In this instance they overlooked both the lady and the talents of an American footballer, to their very great cost."

"You buy the drug idea, then," Peter said.

"Oh, yes indeed. As it happens, Peter, you have a strong supporter for your theory. Constable Pettibone came to the same conclusions that you did and passed them on to me a day or two ago."

"Is something going to happen?"

Winston stopped to look carefully at Kincaid and then at Peter.

"You can count on that," he said.

CHAPTER 32

At an even, smooth five knots, the ocean-going yacht slid slowly through the water toward her mooring at the Bay of Islands. Even to those who had no interest in boats, she was beautiful; her trim, pointed bow sliced the water with hardly a ripple of bow wave, a tribute to the perfection of her design. In an easy, gentle turn she coasted up to her mooring and stopped beside it as though it were hers by some imperial right. Her crew made her fast and went through the routine of shutting her down and securing her, while owners and operators of lesser craft realized that her dignity and grace were beyond their resources.

Four men came off her with an assortment of luggage. They loaded it onto a dolly they had brought with them and set off for the Duke of Marlborough, a little tired but relaxed after their time at sea.

At the end of the pier one of the four, who was quite young, took two heavy suitcases off the dolly, unlocked a parked car, and put them in the rear seat area; they were too large to fit in the trunk of the small vehicle. Just in case anyone was watching—and in Russell that was close to a certainty—he shook hands with the others, stretched his body for a moment, and then climbed in behind the wheel. As the other three continued on toward the hotel, he started the engine easily and drove with proper care through the small town toward the road south.

He was very much at ease. Everything had gone perfectly; even such possible contingencies as a failure of the car to start had been avoided. Now the success of the whole operation was in his hands, and he welcomed the responsibility.

All he had to do was to drive to Auckland, which was not too far away, and deliver the merchandise entrusted to him. He had no cause for concern. The tank was full of petrol. The tires were new, and the spare was properly inflated if it came to that. The car was conventional and inconspicuous, a rental unit no different from a great many others.

When he had arrived at his destination, he would be paid a thousand dollars for his easy work, plus an additional bonus to keep his mouth shut. The only risk he faced was a possible traffic accident, so he drove with maximum care. He was still congratulating himself on his secure position when he turned a corner and found a tall, uniformed figure standing in his way. Behind the man an official car was canted across the narrow road so that he could not get by.

A sudden cold sweat burst out on his body. He could not imagine why he was being stopped, but almost at once he knew what he must do. He had to be a law-abiding motorist ready to cooperate with whatever the policeman asked. In that way he would attract the least amount of attention. He had an international driving license available for inspection. It was a forgery with a false name, but it was so well done, it would pass any but the most rigorous inspection. In the organization for which he worked, details like that were always efficiently handled.

He pulled up and stopped. As the tall man advanced toward him, he leaned out his open window and asked, "What is it, officer?" in a definite American accent.

He had seen the policeman before. He was an old fellow,

probably kept on for the sake of his pension long past the time of his real usefulness. The driver was twenty-four, a hundred and eighty pounds on a six-foot frame, and in fine physical condition. At the same time, he knew that to get into any kind of an altercation with a police officer was the most dangerous thing he could do. That would only be a last resort.

"Good afternoon, sir," Pettibone said. "I'd appreciate it if you'd be kind enough to step out of your car for a moment."

The driver complied, doing what any good citizen would. "What's the problem?" he asked. "Something wrong with the road ahead?"

"No, sir, I just wanted to exchange a few words with you. I believe you were on that fine boat that came in a short while ago."

The young American smiled. "Yes, I was. She's a beauty, isn't she?"

"Undoubtedly. Were you a member of her crew?"

"Invited guest, actually. Some friends of mine asked me along." He kept his tone friendly and relaxed despite the fact that he was still sweating and his knees had a tendency to shake. He wasn't scared of the old man, but he was a cop and he would have a radio in his car. Or perhaps he wouldn't in this Godforsaken place, but it was a risk he couldn't take.

"There's been a recent crime in this area, and I'm looking for possible witnesses."

So that was it! Miraculously, the sweating stopped, and the young American felt enormous relief. "I've been at sea for the last three days," he volunteered.

The policeman looked disappointed. "Three days?" he repeated.

"Yes, we only planned a short cruise."

"And you were, as you say, only a guest onboard?"

"That's right. Of course, I made a hand here and there when I could. Helped wash the dishes and things like that." He was completely at ease, using the winning personality that had helped him in so many things.

"It must have been a real pleasure, especially in such nice weather."

178

The American grinned. "It sure was."

"Then tell me," Pettibone continued, "if you had only planned such a short cruise, why did you take along two such large and heavy cases? I noticed them when you got off the boat."

A swift sharp sense of terror hit the younger man, and the sweating started up again with a rush. He had no ready excuse at hand, because cars were never stopped like this on the roads in New Zealand—that had been part of his briefing. There was one out he could use, but he would have to sacrifice the merchandise, and that would never be forgiven. The knowledge that it was worth millions made him sweat even more. "They aren't mine," he said. "I was asked to drop them off in town."

Pettibone appeared relieved. "I understand, sir. Then in that case, where is your own bag?"

"Look, officer, what's the problem? You said there's been a crime here. When? If it's within the past three days, I can't help you."

Pettibone did not deign to reply to that. Instead, he suddenly became quite firm. "I should like to have a look at those cases," he said. "With your consent, of course. Then you can be on your way. Otherwise . . ."

The young man was desperate. He could stick to his story that he was an innocent courier, but that would still mean detention and endless questions. It would mean the loss of the merchandise and blow the whole operation out of the water. He would never get away with it, and he would lose his promised pay.

Without warning, he lunged at Pettibone, grabbed his throat with his left hand, and aimed a murderous right cross at his jaw. He was young and strong, and he had hit people before. He had also spent some time in the martial arts dojos of Hong Kong.

His blow was blocked by what seemed to be a steel bar. Pettibone spun to the left to break the neck hold and seized the American's wrist. The young man was spun off his feet and slammed hard, face down, onto the pavement. For a moment the wind was out of him; by the time he recovered, he had been expertly handcuffed.

It was hopeless then. He allowed himself to be pushed into the back of the official car because he couldn't help it. His two heavy suitcases were transferred to the back of the police vehicle, his own car was moved to the side, and he was on his way back to Russell. He had scraped his cheek on the pavement and it was bleeding, but he could do nothing about it. He knew without making an attempt that the rear doors of the police car would not open from the inside.

At the police station he was put in the detention room. That done, Pettibone carried in the two cases and inspected their contents. Then he reached for the direct-line telephone and requested assistance. He didn't have adequate facilities to hold four prisoners overnight, and he was a practical man.

CHAPTER 33

As he turned off the main road into the entrance to his station, Peter felt a strong sense of peace. He stopped in the parking area and looked across the lawn at the ranch house. Some of the repair work had already been done, so that the appearance of the building was much improved. Louise stood in the doorway, waiting to welcome him back.

He strode across the grass, feeling with every step that it was his own property, and held out his hands to her. The way she took them gave him a clue; he gathered her in and kissed her warmly, not caring who might be watching.

When he let her go, she asked, "Did you see Dad?"

"Yes," he answered. "He was more comfortable this morning. He was sitting up in bed, and we had a good talk." He stopped to examine the new woodwork on one side of the doorway. It was clearly a first-class job. On the left, the burned boards were still starkly blackened; obviously they hadn't been touched. "When will they finish up?" he asked.

Louise came to stand beside him. "I need a decision from the owner," she said. "Most of the boards can be repainted as they are. The damage is fairly minor, and the appearance should be all right. Or if you want to spend the money, they can all be replaced and no trace of the fire will be left."

"This is a beautiful house," Peter told her. "Why spoil it for the sake of a few dollars?"

"I was sure you'd say that, but I thought I ought to wait and ask you first."

He followed her into the kitchen where she turned and asked, "Tea or coffee?"

"Coffee, and that's all. I ate in Queenstown before I came out. The people at the Mountaineer asked me to say hello."

"Sit down and tell me everything," Louise said. "I'm very anxious to know." She took a pot of hot water off the stove and poured it into a coffee maker.

Peter drew a chair up to the big table. "Thanks for managing everything so well."

Louise concerned herself with the coffee machine until she was able to draw out two cups. "Let's go in the other room," she suggested.

In the large living room the windows were open. Bird songs could be heard with a sharp clarity, reminding Peter how much he had changed his life from the urban environment he had always known. They sat down together on a long sofa, the coffee in front of them.

"How did things go in Wellington?" Louise asked.

Something in her tone told him how to shape his answer. "Very well—in fact, it could hardly have been any better."

"I'm glad to hear that." Then for a brief moment she hesitated. "Did you talk to Ray O'Malley?"

"You mean about Jenny. Yes, I did. You've heard, then."

Louise inclined her head. "Jenny and I have been close friends for a long time," she said. "She called me when she'd made up her mind."

Peter looked at her carefully, studying the planes and contours on her face. "When was that?" he asked.

"Just before you left. I was sick about it, Peter, because I knew you cared for her, but I didn't dare to tell you."

"I'm glad you didn't," he reassured her. "Ray explained to me that Jenny and his son had known each other for years, that this wasn't anything sudden."

"Still, I know it must have hurt you."

"Not too badly. I admit I was attracted to her. She's a stunning girl, and—"

"And she was willing to sleep with you," Louise finished.

He was glad she knew about that—it made things easier. As if to show that she understood, she put her hand on his for a moment. Then she took a little time to drink her coffee. "Jenny, *was* very attracted to you, Peter—in fact, you quite bowled her over. Otherwise she never would have shared a room with you. The thing is, she was already close to committed. I think she was testing herself with a very attractive man. Can you understand that?"

"Of course I can. I'm just grateful she chose me."

Louise gave his hand a little squeeze. "Now, tell me all about Wellington: I want to know everything that happened."

"A lot of it is about Pricane, which wouldn't interest you."

"Yes, it will. I want to know everything that went on."

Peter drank some coffee; then he gave her a condensed account of the meeting in Minister Cooper's office and the conclusions he had offered. She listened silently but with visible interest. When he had finished, she had a comment. "You were right—I know it. That's why they attacked us here and I had to shoot two of them."

"When I told your father about that, he said to me, 'I didn't teach her to miss.' "

"The police were here," Louise said. "Bill Woodley asked me for a full statement, and I gave him one. He phoned the next day and told me to forget it. He said it was clearly self-defense and the matter was closed. Riley was taken to Christchurch to stand trial for the attempted murder of a policeman. After that, there's a charge of murder laid against him in Russell."

"Then I don't get to testify that you saved my life?"

Louise smiled. "I guess not. What kept you so long in Wellington?"

"It seems I'm still working for the ministry of tourism, and they wanted to discuss some things. They're giving serious consideration to the idea of a new hotel at the Bay of Islands. There's a site where it won't destroy any part of the spectacular scenery and will allow more people to enjoy it. If they do build the hotel, it will be a hundred percent New Zealand operation."

"Will you be involved in that?"

"It's possible, because they want to appeal to Americans and I'm one of the principal design engineers at Swarthmore and Stone. For the present, though, I'd much rather just stay here."

"There's a lot to do," Louise said. "Managing a station like this is a big job."

She made a show of finishing her coffee, even though it was by then cold. "What will happen to Kincaid?" she asked. "I'm not so sure he's as innocent as he claimed. He could have ordered the attack on us here. He sounds the kind of man who might do it."

"I thought that too," Peter said, "but however much he was or wasn't involved, it's all over now. He's finished here, and he's finished at Pricane. He's worse off because he's been in Brazil for years and doesn't have any contacts he can turn to in the States. He'll get something eventually, but he may not have a lot of choices."

"Peter, is all big business like that?"

"Pretty much so, I guess. I've had enough of it."

"Good! When are you going back to Wellington?"

"When they send for me. We've agreed on a part-time schedule; I'll go when I'm wanted. Meanwhile, I'm depending on you to teach me the ranching business."

Louise, for reasons of her own, changed the topic. "Are you sure you don't want something to eat?"

"I'm sure." He looked around him at the big, airy, well-furnished room, focusing his mind on what he wanted to say. "Can I be serious for a moment?"

"Of course."

"I enjoyed my time with Jenny very much—any man would—but don't be surprised if I tell you that the news of her engagement didn't mow me down. It was unexpected, but I recovered quite quickly."

"Don't ever tell her that!"

"Of course not. You see, before I went to Wellington, I had time to do a lot of thinking, and only part of it was about all these things that have been going on. Naturally I thought quite a bit about Jenny, but I never got to the point where I felt that I couldn't wait to see her again."

He paused, planning how to shape his words. "For a while I couldn't figure that out. Then, without thinking about it at all, I realized that I wasn't in love with her. I think I sensed that she was already taken. Just as I was."

Louise gasped and a hand flew up in front of her face. "Peter, you never told me!"

"I've never told anybody. Partly because I didn't know it myself until recently. And when I realized what was happening, I knew what had to be and nothing else would ever do." He looked at his companion. "Do you understand me?" he asked.

"I think so," she answered, but her face denied her words.

Seeing that, he took a different tack. He spoke very simply. "I couldn't wait to get back here, where you were. When I held you outside, I didn't ever want to let go. I wanted to keep on holding you indefinitely. Do you understand now?"

"But Jenny—"

"She's got someone to hold her. She should be happy."

"Peter, I—" She broke down, unable to finish. He reached out, drew her beside him, and said calmly, "Take your time."

It took her a full minute before she was ready to talk again. Then she straightened herself up and spoke quite calmly. "I like you, Peter, very much. But partly because of Jenny—" She stopped and started over again. "It's just that—we haven't known each other very long, have we?"

"No," Peter answered her, "but we will. Let me put it this way: Will you be my girl in the meantime? Until you're as certain as I am."

"If you want me to."

As he stood up, Louise rose with him. He put his arms around her and kissed her again. For the first time in his entire life he saw the fulfillment of everything he had ever wanted.

She reached up and put a hand on his shoulder. Despite himself he winced a little; it was still very tender. "I'm sorry," she said. "I'd forgotten."

"No matter at all. I was glad for your hand."

"Maybe you ought to rest for a while. You must have been up early to catch your flight."

"Yes, I was. And I didn't sleep much last night. I had too much on my mind. Mainly you."

He paused and considered her idea. "I think I will lie down for a bit. So far it's been quite a day."

They stood looking at each other for a moment; then Louise spoke. "If you just want to rest for a while, would you like some company?"

He had to hold fast to control the emotion that that simple question aroused in him. It had been so totally unexpected.

"More than I can say," he answered.

She held out her hand, giving of herself. He took it gently and firmly as they walked together across the room toward the fine old staircase.